GHOST TOWNS

LAST STAND

EPISODE TWO

BLAZE WARD

KNOTTED ROAD PRESS

Also by Blaze Ward

First Centurion Kosnett

Encounter at Vilahana

Consensus at Aditi

Hegemony at Dalou

Princes at Ewin

Empire at Gloran

Domain at Yaumgan

The Jessica Keller Chronicles

Auberon

Queen of the Pirates

Last of the Immortals

Goddess of War

Flight of the Blackbird

The Red Admiral

St. Legier

Winterhome

Petron

CS-405

Queen Anne's Revenge

Packmule

Persephone

Additional Alexandria Station Stories

The Story Road

Siren

Two Bottles of Wine With A War God

The Science Officer Series Season One

The Science Officer

The Mind Field

The Gilded Cage

The Pleasure Dome

The Doomsday Vault

The Last Flagship

The Hammerfield Gambit

The Hammerfield Payoff

The Bryce Connection

The Science Officer Series Season Two

Alien Seas

Buried Among the Stars

Captain Navarre

Captain Daring

Revoked

Returned

Reborn

The Lazarus Alliance

Escape

Return

Hunter Bureau

Mirrors

Latency

Pleasure Model

Inhuman

Fairchild

Fairchild

Strawberry Dragon

Background: The Last Stand

A while back, there was a discussion on social media about the short-lived TV show *Firefly*. Six episodes and one movie. Fantastic casting, when you look at the careers of everyone involved, but it died pretty early on the vine, though not without making a major cultural impact.

However…

More recently, unflattering things have come out about the man behind the show. Bad things. Really bad things that I won't repeat here, but a lot of folks no longer have any respect for the man, myself included.

Part of the original discussion involved the fact that the main character (seen from 20 years later) really is something of an asshole to everyone, because the *"creative genius creator and producer"* did a Marty Stu and put himself directly into the show. In turn, folks asked what that show might have been like without that character, and without that asshole in charge.

Two days later, write-brain hit me with *"This is what it looks like…"*

Pull out the original main character, and the sidekick and

"

pilot characters suddenly become central. Keep everyone else, but pull a couple of fast gender swaps to end up with a crew that is (technically: the best kind of correct) six females and two males, one of whom is happily married and kept and the other of whom only sleeps with girls he picks up in bars.

For the setting, I also want to gag at people who set things in the post-civil-war United States, especially when we're supposed to be rooting for the traitors. I have no doubt that, had the television series gone to season three, our main character would have donned a white hood and turned into a science fiction version of Nathaniel Bedford Forrest. In all the bad ways. Icky. Burning crosses or something equally *subtle.*

So I had to change things up, if I was going to have fun with this.

First off, I had to change the background of the setting itself.

David Drake (*Hammer's Slammers* and many other series) studied a LOT of history and reads Latin in the original to translate Ovid, among other things. His creative style was to take actual historical events and settings and twist them around some for his space opera. I needed to do the same.

For the Last Stand series, I started with a review of Napoleonic Europe, but with one, critical, historical difference. Instead of Napoleon destroying his army invading Russia, he won, conquering the Russian Empire (and functionally all of the European landmass) and eliminating the Russian aristocratic class. Or rather, swapping out most of them, as the serfs didn't see any difference.

For Tessa, my main character, badass, amazon, warrior babe, I also used Russian history. In her case, I based her on a taller version of (model/actress/etc.) Zhanna Zhumaliyeva. Gorgeous. Kazakh, because in the early part of the nineteenth century, the Russian Empire was pushing south into the Black Sea area and conquering (and often wiping out) all of the tribes and nations that had previously lived there. That formed the basis of the Vlikine.

Similarly, I needed the include a touch of the German Principalities (Altenfeld), mostly because they all got conquered by Napoleon but not absorbed in our history before Wellington and Friends sent the Corsican packing. Twice.

Swiss neutrality got included in a more modern conception of Inleah, where they would happily sell anything to anyone with cash in hand. Always cash up-front. Mercenary to an amoral fault. Tessa's husband Fin is from Inleah. And all he ever wants to do was fly.

Ergrove is my British Empire, with all the foibles and charm of the original, pushed forward into space and twisted around. Some nice things. Some not so nice things. More accurate, if you will.

Imperial France becomes Lorastir, the height of culture and sophistication, as Napoleonic France tended to be in those days. Wyatt and Laney both served in the Lorastir army, neither of them in the infantry, if you will, but I won't spoil some of the surprises coming your way.

There was a character in the television series who was everyone's favorite, because she was a modern geisha. Educated. Eloquent. Beautiful. The series literally treated her like a whore, abusing her to no end in ways that any woman worth her salt wouldn't have put up with from any other screen writer.

I got lucky. Way lucky.

As a writer, I have friends. Some are peers. Some are folks I mentor. One of the latter is someone I refer to as Renaissance Babe™ because she's been a concert pianist, photographer, writer, and had to retire as a nude model when she turned 30 because she had *aged out*. (Dumbasses.)

In Abigail, I created the Players. Geisha as they really were, rather than the fancy prostitutes that western media have since made them out to be. Raconteurs, chefs, musicians. Sex might be on the menu, if they like you, but maybe you hire them to come in and cook an incredible meal, then sit and talk for hours.

My Renaissance Babe™ was an invaluable resource for creating Abigail, because she has literally been in those situations and could offer expert advice on how to fix things I got initially wrong. I considered it the highest compliment when she told me that she wants to be Abigail when she grows up. Better, she took the concept of the Player, and is working on telling her own set of stories with something similar. Not many people could get all those little details right.

There are no original stories. There are only original takes. New ways to see a character or a setting. I'm utterly thrilled that I have inspired her to go off on this tangent, since my work here was a tangent on the original set of complaints about how badly that television show holds up, twenty years later. (Go watch the first triple episode without the blinkers and get back to me before you comment. You will be appalled at the behavior.)

Finally, the two fugitives. I got what the original creator was doing, but my plan with this series is to not have paranormal abilities running around, just as there won't be aliens. (That latter is because I don't need to deal with the extra complexities of colonialism and all the bad things that arise on both sides of that equation. Conscious decision here, so that the stories are human ones.)

I liked the fugitive doctor, but had to twist it. Made him a woman. She rescued her sister, and then bought a pair of identities that list them as husband and wife, because everyone is looking for two women. Constanz and Brianna McLaren.

This lets her hide in plain sight, as it were, while dealing with the fact that she is a woman. And she only *presents* as male to hide. She won't get to be girly all that often, but occasionally it will peek out, as it were.

The sister, Brianna, is described as one of the most beautiful women you will ever encounter, taking her natural beauty and augmenting it. At the same time, they broke her mind. And she has spent years trying to reassemble it with Constanz's help. And now, with the crew of the Last Stand.

Finally, the series itself.

In my mind, each of these novellas is intended to represent one hour of television time, with commercial breaks. That is, 42 minutes of screen, including opening and closing credits.

Once upon a time, I wrote dramas for the stage. Then I worked on screenplays (I have several, if you have a few million bucks burning a hole in your pocket, BTW.)

A screenplay reads as just about one minute of screen for one page of dialogue, depending. When I started writing the original Science Officer books, that was in the back of my mind, because forty minutes of screen works out to roughly 22,000-24,000 words of fiction. Thus, the novella.

The Last Stand series are all novellas. Episode #1/**Lost Dreams**, is longer, but that's me introducing the world and whole cast in an extra-long episode. So far, with one exception (I have nine in the can), they all come in around 22,000 words, which was my target. Enough story to have a singular conflict and resolve it, plus side stories and details to give it depth.

Better, because I have a large cast, I can focus each story on a different character and really show you who they are. One of my first readers complained about #5 because she understood the situation and agreed with me that Tessa's solution was perfectly correct, but it irritated her, because the more she thought about it, none of her (First Reader's) alternatives would work. That means I got her all the way down into the best kind of ethical conundrum, where there are only less-bad solutions to be had.

My (current) plan is to publish one of these stories each month in 2023. That's twelve episodes, which makes a nice Season One and then lets me take a break and step back. I have some thirty possible plots I could work with, plus whatever I come up with going forward. I have nine of them in the can, as mentioned, and I already know what #11 and #12 will be. (Both circle back to earlier stories and expand them in new, fun ways.)

As with the Science Officer, I don't know what Season Two will look like. I like to work with novellas at this length because I can write them quickly. With Science Officer, I bumped up to full novels with Season Two, because I wanted to tell bigger stories there. Here? Remains to be seen.

I'm having fun. And my first readers have all noticed the fun. I did not slavishly follow the original run of the television show and movie. In fact, I watched that first triple episode to see what they had done (and how badly it held up) so I could create more interesting and in-depth versions of the characters as I twisted them around.

Personally, I'm not sure if the television characters would have ever gotten any great depth to them. The man behind it all appears to be something of a sexist, homophobic, racist punk, if you listen to all the horror stories that have come out. There are stories about him and his buddies have competitions to see who could make a young, new, female writer cry first. Talk about toxic workplace.

Instead, I wanted to create rich people. Deep. Complex. And not cardboard cutouts. Some of the stories are 100%

action from bowsprit to sternlights, but some of them are slower burns, diving deep into the ethics of a world where the heroes occasionally have to rob banks. And regularly smuggle illegal goods from place to place.

That's similar to the world we live in today, when the wealthy have grown their political power desperately out of scale with the economy and the rest of the world. If nothing changes, there will be a terrible collapse at some point, simply because the world can't handle this imbalance.

So come, join me on an adventure into Hawkwold Sector and follow the crew as they take Last Stand into dark places and light ones, meeting dukes and scoundrels, governors and warlords.

Tessa isn't about to take any shit, and she's got a crew full of dangerous friends who will help her out.

Shade and sweet water,

b

West of the Mountains, WA

20221110

Scene One

Tessa had been up on the bridge reading all morning, mostly to escape the noise and people down in the commons and the kitchen area. Wasn't that she didn't like everyone aboard, even as her new passengers were turning into something of a longer-term gig than she'd originally imagined.

Some days, however, they were all breathing her air, and that was a mite much to handle, so she'd evicted her husband and taken the co-pilot chair with her Personal Analytical Engine and a pot-boiling bodice-ripper scroll some previous passenger had left behind. Even going into town to buy something new for the ship's library had sounded like too much work.

Instead, she'd closed the forward shades three-quarters for a bit better ambiance than the bright, noonday sun of *Newhall's* Astoria, and read after breakfast.

She'd been sitting too long. Stiff. Had to go pee. Gonna have to face people.

She uncoiled the spring on her Analytical Engine and slipped it into a handy drawer for later. Wasn't the first time she'd read this one. Hadn't been that interesting then, either. Enough to while away the time.

But she'd needed to move about for a bit. Got her lazy ass up and headed down the stairs to the rest of the ship. Paused in her quarters for personal relief, then meandered farther aft, past the McLarens each reading on their own, fancier Analytical Engines, brought with them from the Arles Region. The gravitational center of civilization so far from the Hawkswold Sector where Tessa lived.

They both looked up and nodded, but she kept going. Tea sounded good about now.

Which was how she found her husband Fin, bent over the big dining table, humming to himself and studying some map Tessa didn't recognize. Huge, maybe a meter tall by two long and not contained in the usual three-ring binder where nav records of every star system were usually kept.

Auntie Maru, Tessa's real aunt Marusya but everyone called her Auntie these days, was sitting nearby, sipping tea. She had a look in her eyes like a lifeguard over a pool as Fin worked. Never a good sign. From the sounds, Wyatt and Laney were aft in the cargo bay lifting weights and spotting each other.

Tessa went ahead and got the makings for tea.

Fin didn't even look up at her.

Steeped it and stood there, looming beside him.

He finally sniffed the air and turned to her.

"Oh, hi."

She rolled her eyes in his general direction, exactly matching Maru doing the same.

"You've been out here the longest," Fin continued, standing up now and stretching with creaks like she had. "Ever hear of a planet named *Lacot*?"

Tessa supposed that she had been in this space more than anyone else, mostly because you couldn't ever get a straight answer out of Wyatt Nakada to that question. He liked having that ambiguous and maybe compelling mysterious backstory.

Tessa assumed old bench warrants for traffic fines or something.

Still, she sipped her tea and considered Fin's question. And how he associated her with a particular smell of tea. Then she realized that nobody else aboard drank that flavor.

Huh.

Her husband was weird. Lovable goofball who was happily kept, but weird.

"*Lacot?*" she asked. "Hawkswold Sector?"

He turned back to the paper on the table and a finger came down on a spot.

"According to this," he said. "But I've checked my books and don't see any coordinates or references to it."

That seemed to cause the gravity of the ship to shift, drawing her over to stand next to him.

Starmap, but all on one big page, so every system had a right ascension, declination, and distance from the capital at *Beaumonde*. With at least one extra she'd never heard of.

Lacot. Way the hell out on the perimeter of a Periphery sector, which meant the middle of bloody nowhere as far as that went. Out near the edges of known and explored space.

Humanity was largely centered on the Arles Region, containing Lorastir's newly enlarged Empire, plus Ergrove, Inleah, and a variety of much smaller nations. Outside that, a bunch of tiny places, generally removed from the core, about half of which were either owned or dominated by Ergrove these days. Even Chen, well beyond her own home in Zaddinul, was having trouble keeping Ergrove merchants and adventurers from messing things up.

Lacot was nowhere. Utterly nowhere. Nobody even close.

Tessa set her tea down off to one side and bent over to

get a closer look, unsurprised when Fin's hand found her bottom.

"Keeping you from falling over," he nodded with wide-eyed helpfulness.

"Uh huh," she grunted.

Auntie was back to rolling her eyes, with a wider target now.

The map was old. Had that old paper, musty smell and starting to yellow with passing decades. And the lettering had been done by hand. Good hand, but this thing had never come out of a printer, mechanical or electronic.

There were other stars out there. This slice of the galaxy was pretty dense, compared to the gaps on either side of the arm. At the same time, none of the neighbors were marked inhabited or even explored.

Just *Lacot*, out there alone in the darkness.

She stood up, again unsurprised that her husband kept hold of her bottom. It was a nice bottom. She walked and worked out enough to assure that. He liked to touch it to remind her how much he appreciated it. She pretty much always rolled her eyes at that.

She didn't tower over him, but still stood a hand taller. About ten centimeters. He was a little short. She was a lot tall. Skinny guy, athletic girl, with his sandy blond hair a little long to go with a precisely trimmed mustache and Van Dyke and a ready smile. Blue-green eyes.

Tessa was Vlikine originally. Back before that tribe had largely been wiped out by Zaddinul nobles looking for new planets to own. Dark olive skin. Wide, flat face. Black hair. Dark eyes.

Scars, but only some of them were visible.

"Thoughts?" she asked.

"Snipe hunt," he replied with a knowing nod.

Her confusion must have shown.

"Maybe it's a real place," he nodded. "Maybe this map is out of a fantasy book or something, and they added a make-believe place, like *Barakzir*, where your legendary King Fyodor would come back from in Zaddinul's time of need. That sort of thing."

Fantasy was right. King Fyodor hadn't ridden up with his magical sword to save Zaddinul from Lorastir. Or anybody else.

Tessa was hard pressed to say if it would have made any measurable difference in the lives of anybody but the wealthy nobles. The serfs had just changed masters for the most part.

"M'kay," she nodded back at him.

"So one of these days, maybe we get a job that puts us out there and we can swing by and see if it really exists," Fin said brightly.

"Where'd you get this?" she asked.

"Laney found it in a book she found in town," Fin said, maybe a little defensively. "A real book, in a junk store down at the left end. Book was nothing but old Ergrove love poetry, badly written, but somebody had folded up this map and stashed it inside. Shopkeeper didn't want the book that bad, and hadn't found the map, so she bought it and brought it here. Asked me to look at it."

Huh. Sure, weirder shit had happened. And Tessa vaguely knew of the shop Fin was referencing, though she and the crew were fairly new to *Newhall* and the town of Astoria outside the port. Up until recently, *Last Stand* had been mostly based out of *Alfann* and Weinsefeld Docks.

New world. For everybody.

"Should I ask around about a cargo that takes us in that general direction as an excuse?" Tessa asked.

She liked the way Fin's pretty blue eyes lit up at that. He never asked her for much. Man wanted to fly more than anything in life, and it had gotten him all the way out to

Hawkswold Sector and away from his safe, pretty home in neutral Inleah.

Tessa nodded and leaned down to kiss him. Last job had paid pretty well, so they were even a little ahead on things around here, plus a mass of paying passengers.

And she hadn't had anything approaching a vacation in years. A ship like this always needed maintenance, especially as old as it was. Plus, it was Zaddinul manufacture, so parts were hard to find, due to weird styling and measurements compared to Ergrove standards. And a Zaddinul soul, so sometimes a pain in the ass, but it would never surrender.

Rather like someone else Tessa knew.

"I'll go talk to Bao Li and see what she might be able to find for us," Tessa assured him. "You and Laney maybe head into town and see if you can find anything else that might help solve that mystery while we're gone?"

"On it," he said, immediately moving to fold up the map then stash it in the book she'd ignored earlier, sitting out of place on the dining table.

Auntie Maru immediately rose as well, mug in hand, nodding as if to say she would have the engines and systems ready to go, if Tessa decided to depart after dinner.

She had a good crew. And good passengers turning into friends.

It was a little weird, but maybe, just maybe, things were turning in her favor finally.

Scene Two

"You want to go where?"

Tessa had been expecting the blowback from Bao Li. Woman was a fixer and a broker. A local power broker in Astoria and the whole *Newhall* system. And even seemed to like Tessa, though beyond sharing a gender, Tessa would be hard pressed to say why.

Unless moxie counted.

"*Parth*," Tessa repeated. "Got some business out that way and it would be nice not to have to deadhead the run."

Bao Li's restaurant was a top-notch place, but absolutely dead this afternoon. Private club, which was a nice way of saying gangster establishment where tourists weren't allowed in, with expected bribes for cops and health inspectors to generally leave the woman and her staff alone.

Bao Li was in her usual booth, with Tessa across from her enjoying an iced rum sour and the requisite bouncers close in case they needed to bodily throw Tessa out the front door.

"There is nothing in *Parth*, Captain Sladek," Bao Li assured her. "Hell, I'm always amazed when I find out that there are still people living there."

"Why's that?" Tessa asked, curious.

"Hot and dry, even in the nice parts," Bao Li nodded. "Too close to their star. Fools tried to raise grain at one point, but you got to move a shit ton of a cargo like that to be profitable. No mining worth a bag of beans, because iron and nickel are available in any damned asteroid you want to waylay. What are you really up to, Sladek?"

"I'd rather not say, ma'am," Tessa replied a bit evasively, unsure if she would set herself up for ridicule or competition, were she to tell the woman anything approaching the truth. "As I said, headed out that direction, hoping to find a cargo to offset my daily expenses. If they're farmers and miners, maybe some secondhand luxury goods you want to move for gold-plated prices?"

"Hell, they don't have the gold to afford anything," Bao Li laughed. "Unless you want to convert your whole cargo hold to hauling grain. And most of that is hauled in ships with cargo bays bigger than *Last Stand*."

Tessa shrugged. Sipped her lovely drink. Ice meant the total amount of alcohol involved was barely enough to count. Mostly moisture and flavor, which was good enough.

Tessa had never developed expensive tastes.

"You're serious, aren't you?" the woman asked after a moment.

Tessa nodded. Words unspoken here wouldn't be tools against her later, so she kept her mouth shut and smiled.

"Okay, let me look around," Bao Li said after a moment. "Doubt you'd do more than break even on something like that, but as you said, the alternative is a deadhead run."

"Thank you kindly," Tessa said.

She took that for the dismissal it was and slipped out of the booth, standing between the big bruisers and nodding to Qulu Azad, Bao Li's executive assistant. Or whatever she called the young man.

Dog robber might be as good a term, as he didn't look like a boy toy the middle-aged woman kept around for physical needs. Brains, when the rest of the folks in here were brawn, not counting two bored waiters and an eye-candy woman tending bar.

"You are up to no good, Sladek," Bao Li called when Tessa was halfway to the door.

Tessa paused and turned back.

"Maybe," she offered. "But it was my husband's idea and he hardly ever asks for things."

Bao Li looked utterly befuddled at that, but Tessa wasn't going to explain in any better detail.

What was love, after all, but doing silly things for someone?

Scene Three

Fin didn't do adventure much. Well, beyond crazy flying because the law or a dumbass, would-be pirate had opinions on some topic they wanted to share.

If they could catch him.

None had yet. Tessa didn't count.

Goal in life was keeping that streak going as long as he could.

Since it had been Laney's book originally, he'd asked her to accompany him for a second trip to town. Wyatt, looking bored, had tagged along. Fin felt tiny compared to the pair of them, considering how much taller both were, and how much combined mass they carried.

Still, he was perfectly safe around here, unless someone brought an entire army with them. And maybe then, too.

Wyatt, however, sounded like an eight-year-old at times.

"Why are we doing this?" the big man asked as they got to the main market square and turned right this time.

Laney's book had been left when she'd gone exploring yesterday and cleaned out that end of town. Today, he was going right to keep things balanced. Or off-balance, as it were. Never let them see you coming.

"Might be more information," Fin said. "Maybe an old history book that will or won't prove anything."

"And here I thought you'd need me," Wyatt grumped.

"I'm sure there will be things on top shelves I can't reach," Fin assured him.

"I do more than that," Wyatt replied.

"Yes, but I doubt I'll need anyone to open a jar of pickles until we get back to the ship. Or were you hoping somebody tried to mug us in broad daylight again?"

Wyatt fell silent. Laney gave both of them a good case of side-eye, but wisely kept her questions to herself. Wyatt was great at shooting things. Fin needed him because he was tall. And good at opening jars.

It was a thing.

Fin paced, measuring shops by façades for something he couldn't really explain. There were a couple of used bookstores around here, mostly because folks needed to trade out scrolls for their Analytical Engines regularly.

Laney, however, had found a real book in a junk store. Printed in a factory. Bound and glued. Filled with love poetry bad enough that Fin would have been embarrassed to attach his name, but obviously someone had liked it enough to go to that expense.

Bookstores didn't sound right to his way of thinking. If nothing else, they would have both found that map and kept it. Or sold it separately. Laney had been in one of the local junk stores, but one serving permanent natives, rather than folks passing through.

Maybe that was it? Not sailors. Or maybe an ex-sailor. Ex-farmer, given up her dreams on *Lacot* and made it back as far as *Newhall*? Settle in a town like Astoria and call it good enough? Die here, and folks at whatever boarding house hauled your stuff off and pawned it?

Fin nodded and lengthened his stride. Laney stayed right with him as he swooped through post-lunch crowds. Wyatt caught up shortly.

"You have an idea?" Laney asked.

"I have a crazy vision," Fin grinned back at her. "Not the same thing."

The woman laughed. It was the sound of someone who has been there, and done that.

Fin had been thinking to hit stores from the middle and work his way down, but now he changed his mind and went clear to the farthest end of the strip. Until the road ended and he was looking at open scrub prairie, the sort of place where there was just enough rain most of the time to keep grass.

On either side of him, boardwalks ended in such a way that Fin found himself looking around for the signs reading "Here There Be Dragons" as a warning.

He turned his back on the wilderness and considered his options.

"If I lived in a boarding home, like these sorts of buildings, I'd largely stay away from the center of town," he opined aloud. "Town is basically two blocks wide on this side of the docks, and ten kilometers long, not counting the palace complex that sits off the back like a bubble."

"Okay," Laney said.

Wyatt scowled at the thin crowd like he might cow them into submission. Those that bothered to pay any attention to the man.

"And if I died one night, folks would steal what might be worth stealing, then haul the rest off as junk for a few jiao coins," Fin continued. "Where would I go?"

"Hell, according to most of the preachers I've ever

known," Wyatt laughed. "But my shit would end up in the second door on the left in the meantime."

"Why's that?" Fin asked, looking up at the big man, a bit surprised.

Fin knew that Wyatt was smarter than he let on. Most of the man was an act, either to get you to ignore him, or underestimate him.

"Joint for locals," Wyatt nodded, already walking that way. "Sailors and ruffians aren't welcome."

Fin glanced at Laney and followed.

Wyatt sure was acting funny if that was a place where folks like them weren't supposed to go.

Scene Four

Fin followed the big man into the shop. Crowded space, with tall shelves on all sides overflowing with the detritus of many lives that he would need Wyatt to grab down for him. If any of it was interesting.

"Help you find something?" a fussy little man behind the counter perked up as they entered. Ancient, from the roadmap of wrinkles around his eyes.

"Books," Fin said, playing it by ear for the most part. "Old stuff. Doing research and don't think the other shops would have what I need."

"What did you need?" the man asked sharply.

Tiny. Ancient. Eyes like a dragon that had just awakened from a nap to find three goofballs accidentally wandering 'round his treasure vaults.

Wyatt and Laney on his flanks just accentuated the look of trouble.

"The history of the sector," Fin explained. "The real one, and not whatever hokum the current governor might have edited this year for his personal edification."

That elicited a laugh, a sharp, barking tone.

"Hawkswold is nearly five centuries old at this point, young man," the elderly shopkeeper noted. "Could you narrow that down?"

"Ghost towns," Wyatt said quietly.

The old man sobered appreciably. So did Fin.

The whole shop fell silent, like a real ghost had just walked in, demanding attention. Fin glanced up at the big man, almost in disbelief.

"That, I believe, is a most interesting term," the keeper finally said.

Fin decided to play a hunch.

"I'm trying to win a bet," he said. Not entirely bullshit, as the bet was with himself, and this man didn't need to know that. "Someone said that the sector started small and has largely grown slowly, like a pearl accreting. I think that maybe it surged and receded a few times. Maybe systems got settled, but things didn't work out. Too hot, too cold, too something. Trying to see what might be out there off the beaten track."

"You're new in town," the man said.

Fin nodded.

"Fin Barton, pilot off the freighter *Last Stand*," he replied. "These two are also part of the crew."

Close enough. Laney had stood with them with guns when she'd had to. And knew secrets folks around these parts might be willing to kill for.

"Looking to open new markets?" the man asked with a knowing smile.

"I wish," Fin laughed. "Figure anything like that is either well known, or overrun with pirates. This is mostly curiosity, unless you happened to know some places where we could haul a small cargo for a profit. Captain's my wife, and she's always open to new gigs."

The man studied them for a long moment, possibly considering. Then he pointed.

"Try down this aisle about midway," he said quietly. "Don't know if it will have what you seek, but it might. Did you bring a reader?"

Fin stopped and blinked at the man.

"No?"

"Not all of them have the case they came in, so sometimes I have to write a brief description on the outside, rather than the blurb they came with," the man said. "If one of those looks interesting, bring it up and I'll load it for you to look at."

"Thank you," Fin replied.

He turned and followed Wyatt down the aisle, Laney trailing.

Real books were rare on the Periphery, unless you had a crapton of money and wanted to show it off. Most folks did fine with a reader. A Personal Analytical Engine.

You loaded it up with a small cartridge about the size of a deck of playing cards. Wound your reader's springs, then advanced to the first page of text. Innards were just a bunch of holes punched in a length of something like plastic, but the reader's mechanical innards turned them into letters.

Electronics were nice, but wore out way too fast. Factories to make new ones were rare and expensive. A good Analytical Engine could be repaired by any tinker worth her salt, and would last for generations if you took care of them.

The books as he looked at them were largely standing, long edge out. Most of them looked like cheap, escapism fantasy fiction. Magic. Romance. Crime. Bizarre alien invasions.

Fin pulled a couple, just to look at the covers, chuckle, and shove them right back in. Depending on the age, most had originally been sold for a jiao or two. All of them went for a few fen today. He grabbed a few at random, just to add to the library on the ship.

"Here," Laney said, drawing his attention down and to a corner he'd missed looking at the nicer stuff. The ones with worn corners from being handled too much that the stock was losing color.

Wyatt loomed. Laney squatted. Fin joined her.

Non-fiction took up half of a shelf, compared to four bookcases' worth of various fiction. Fin wondered what that said about things, but decided that most folks in a place like Astoria would want to be entertained, rather than educated. Probably all of *Newhall*, and however many other planets.

They'd go to *Beaumonde* if they wanted a proper university.

"Nothing on ghost towns," Fin muttered under his breath.

"Couldn't think of a better way to describe them," Wyatt muttered back. "Not without saying too much to the old geezer."

Again, you forgot how smart Wyatt was under that dumb punk exterior. Fellow had a brain. Didn't like using it wasn't the same as not having anything to use.

Fin grabbed a weird case off the corner and flipped it over to read.

Handwritten, rather than the original case.

"Plants You Should Know?" Laney asked.

"Wondering if they list places where you might find them," Fin said. "Plus, could be helpful expanding the hydroponics and herb gardens, if we knew what we were missing."

A run through everything else available didn't turn up anything interesting, but Fin wasn't surprised. If this was where your stuff ended up after you died, it would be the things most valuable to you, generally for sentimental purposes, after you slowly stripped away every single layer of your life.

Down to that last book, maybe.

Like a pearl in reverse.

He stood, carrying the spool like a holy relic from an earlier age. Shopkeeper pulled out his own reader and popped out the cartridge as Fin approached.

Fin placed it in the man's hand and watched him load it. Old man set it on the counter between them and pressed the Advance button several times, a set of clicks that fast forwarded through early stuff to the meat in the middle.

Book even had hand-drawn, black and white sketches to display. Started with tomatoes, which Fin supposed were among the most common and important, since you could can them so easily. *Climate. Growing conditions. Canning.*

There. Fin wanted to point and cry out in triumph, but held himself close and silent.

Places you might find them in the wild.

"How old is this book?" Fin asked, unsure which answer would be best for his needs.

Too modern and they might have forgotten *Lacot,* assuming it ever existed anywhere but somebody's fertile imagination. Too old and folks might not yet have settled out there.

Shopkeeper backed up to the legal page.

"Hunnert years, give or take," he replied, looking at the dates. "Botany mostly moves slow, unless you've got a breeding program on the ship."

"No, but we grow a lot of vegetables and herbs," Fin said. "Hydroponics and pots. Helps things smell nicer, and adds a treat to a meal. Don't have any fruit trees, but part of that is the breeding needs."

"Apples are lovely," the man nodded. "Pain in the ass cross fertilizing. Same with pears. Citrus often works in pots."

"So I've been told," Fin agreed, not willing to explore down that path much.

"You ever trade seeds?" the man asked out of the blue.

Fin glanced up sharply.

"Have," he nodded carefully. "Usually with other ships at one of the big moots, where folks trade canned and jarred goods, plus crafts. We rarely generate enough surplus on the ship, but other folks specialize in things, so we buy with cash."

"Astoria Port is a shallow place," the man said. "Filled mostly with travelers coming and going, but not hanging around much."

"That kind of describes my ship," Fin agreed, uncertain where the man was headed. "We used to be largely based out of *Alfann*, but moved lately to *Newhall*."

"Plenty of folks in the same boat," the man said. "Once you get outside of town, however, *Newhall* is a much nicer place."

"Outside?" Fin asked, thinking back to the endless prairie he'd seen just beyond where that last boardwalk ended.

"You can't hardly see any of it from here," the man laughed. "Next time you take off, if you headed a little more south than east, you might be surprised. Especially at night, when all the lights were on."

"I shall keep that in mind," Fin replied. "How much for the book?"

"Let you have it for two fen," the man nodded. "And maybe you come back sometime with a list of seeds you'd be willing to trade for."

Fin dug into his pocket and found a handful of coins for this one and the couple of others. It was a pretty good deal, but he wouldn't really know if he'd gotten lucky until he got back to the ship and went through the whole thing while taking notes.

Still, he might have made a new friend in town.

And maybe outside of town as well.

SCENE FIVE

Tessa had gotten her goofball husband to help pull the shipping crate of seeds they had originally stolen on *Orvan,* then catalog things into a journal. The new book had helped, mostly by identifying all the plants they didn't have and might want.

"The old man suggested trading seeds?" Tessa confirmed as they finished organizing all the little envelopes on the main table.

Folks had come and gone all afternoon, but mostly were staying in their cabins or forward in the rec room. At least until it came time to fix dinner.

"He thought that the locals would be interested," her husband agreed. "Not the sailors, but everyone always forgets that there's a broader economy in places like Astoria. You've got the shippers and everyone working with or preying on them. Then the government. Finally, the settlers just trying to make a life. He suggested that there were a lot more people outside Astoria than maybe we expected. Or anybody expected."

"Huh," she grunted.

On the one hand, that made perfect sense. On the other, the only time she might go outside of the major shipping points was either to land quietly and sneak up someplace to rob somebody, or if a cargo needed to be picked up or delivered to a ranch in the middle of nowhere.

But *Newhall* was probably a lot like her home at *Nulbuzir* had been, once upon a time.

All those folks you had to dance around on the strip had to come from somewhere, and they weren't all from other ships or whorehouses.

"What else did the old man have for sale?" Tessa asked. "Different from the rest of the pawn shops on the strip."

He'd started to speak, then paused, contemplative-like.

"Crafts," he finally said, lips pressed together in deep thought. "If you had a hobby that didn't involve flying on a ship, or flying a ship, and you needed something to keep you sane. I remember stuff for knitting or making clothes. Tinker's tools and materials for working wood and metal. Art supplies, I suppose, since he had paints in tiny jars rather than buckets you'd need to paint the interior of your house or ship."

"Things to brighten your life," Tessa nodded. "But you have to do it yourself, because you live so far from one of the major worlds with regular cargo shipments that it takes a year or more for something you ordered to arrive."

"*Parth*," he said, eyes lighting up.

"*Parth*," she agreed, leaning in to kiss him. "Bao Li is going to see about getting us a cargo to give us an excuse to make that run, but she doesn't understand what we're up to. Not sure I do, but what if we went back to that old man and cleaned him out of things that a world like *Parth* might find useful?"

"Worst that can happen is one of us ends up having to learn how to knit," Fin said.

"Oh, I can help you with that," Abigail said as she wandered in from forward. "Need a sweater?"

Of course, a Player would have learned all those skills. Finery, yes, but just being able to sit around with a client and knit might be enough to be hired. Telling stories while hands were kept busy.

Much as popular culture liked to paint Players as if they were nothing but jumped-up whores, Tessa knew that Abigail ended up having any sort of carnal relations with less than a third of the folks that hired her.

Most wanted conversationalists able to talk about this and that. Storytellers bringing word from other worlds. Even someone who could cook you a gourmet meal or play a song and sing.

Or sit and knit.

"We're thinking about heading to *Parth*," Tessa told the tiny, beautiful woman. "Hauling a cargo of art supplies and such out to those folks."

"*Parth*?" Abigail wrinkled her pert nose. "Why are you heading all the way out there?"

"You missed the ghost town map Laney found for me," Fin said.

"Ghost town?" Abigail asked dryly, seemingly unconvinced.

"*Lacot*. A planet, supposedly, not on any of my regular nav charts," Fin nodded. "Way out beyond *Parth*. Or at least that's the closest world known to be inhabited right now."

"Never heard of it," Abigail said. "But knitting is easy. Patterns are the hard part, so make sure you pick up a bunch. A whole planet might produce all the wool they need, so patterns would be good to sell. As would dyes. Same with clothing, if you're going down that route."

She paused, staring at them.

Tessa took the opportunity to close her mouth from where it had fallen open in shock. Fin did the same.

"I should make you a list, shouldn't I?" Abigail asked carefully.

"Please?" Fin said.

"How soon did you want to leave?" Abigail asked. "I've not got anything booked right now, but that was mostly the first surge of interest tapering off and me not immediately filling my calendar since you hardly stay on any one planet more than a week."

Tessa felt herself blush. Abigail understood this ship. And this crew.

"We might shop tomorrow," she said. "Get it all delivered by the day after that. Too soon?"

"No," Abigail smiled. "I might take a few days off and just enjoy myself."

She headed over to the kitchenette to make some coffee and Tessa turned to her husband.

"Ghost towns?" Tessa asked quietly.

"Wyatt's term, but you know what? It works," he nodded. "No idea what we might find. Or who. Didn't see *Lacot* in my book of plants, but that doesn't mean anything. Might be too late. Or reprinted from something too early. I'd like to go see. But I also think that *Parth* might be useful. Bao Li was thinking big, expensive things you could make a lot of profit on, wasn't she?"

"She was," Tessa agreed. "Maybe she forgot about the simple folk that make up a world."

"We all do," Fin nodded. "Get so wrapped up in our daily grind that we forget to stop and smell the roses. We should grow roses."

Tessa leaned over and flicked a few bags around until she found the one.

"Find me a pot," she said, holding up seeds.
He grinned.
"Sounds like an adventure."

Scene Six

Tessa had accompanied Fin and Abigail into town this time, mostly because she wanted to see about this new business her silly husband might have accidentally stumbled into. They'd taken the cargo truck, her riding in back with Abigail up front and the windscreen blocking things so the woman's hair was still beautiful.

Tessa settled for hot and heavily armed. It was an entirely different fantasy from the perfection of a woman like Abigail. Still a fantasy for some men.

Fin parked out front and locked the truck down by pulling one of the power relays and stuffing it into his pocket. Tessa had her revolver, but had left the rifle back on the ship. Anyone trying to get to the McLarens would have to go through Wyatt and Laney, so Tessa wasn't all that worried.

Down to the end of the strip, where she could see Fin's poetic description of the end of the line stretched out in front of her, and found herself looking forward to flying out and over there to see more of the planet than she remembered from earlier trips.

They went inside and Tessa adjusted to the dimmer light.

"Ah, you're back," a voice said from her left. "And brought more friends."

She followed Fin that direction.

"This is my wife, Tessa," Fin introduced them. "And Abigail here is a Player who frequently travels with us."

"Ladies, it is a pleasure to make your acquaintance," he said. "I am MacGeorge."

Odd name, but Tessa just smiled. Old fellow. As much as another generation beyond Auntie or Laney, both in their mid-fifties.

"And I brought you something," Fin said, pulling a bag filled with a few sleeves of seeds and placing it on the counter. "We came into a selection recently and hadn't gotten them all planted or traded off. Thought you might be able to make use of them."

Tessa was the tallest person in the room, so she had a clear view as the man lifted the seeds and read the labels Fin had written, his lips moving as he did.

"Most helpful," MacGeorge nodded. "Was there something in particular you were looking for today?"

Tessa glanced around, noting the odd combination of used stuff and what Fin and Abigail had described as art supplies. Things you might need on a farm or ranch in the middle of nowhere, when you got to town on a weekly or even monthly basis, rather than being able to walk to your favorite bar or food truck.

It was an entirely different lifestyle than anything she wanted to try.

"We're headed to *Parth*," Fin was explaining. "Got some business out that way, and wondered if maybe we should clean you out of your art supplies to haul to them. That and seeds, as you noted. Also, did anyone around here have things they might want to send to *Parth*? We're planning to shop today, maybe load tomorrow depending, and then fly out."

MacGeorge nodded.

"I will put out the word in a bit and see if folks need mail hauled," he said. "As for now, let's take a look at what you saw. I can offer some suggestions as to what value it might have on a world like *Parth*."

Tessa wandered around to look at things, leaving the other three to touch things and chatter in a vocabulary so esoteric as to almost be a cant. Outside, she could nearly see a line in the dirt separating the port folks from the people just living here. Many of those worked in shops and bars, but never traveled.

Maybe only stayed for a time as seasonal workers, before heading back out to some farm or village out over the horizon? She'd never given it a lot of thought, other than flying over and shaking her head at the choices some folks made.

But out there was a thick line, fading between one color and the next, demarcating worlds. Somehow, Laney and her dear, goofball husband had wandered across it, like stepping into a fairy ring, then made it home safe.

At least she hoped so. Weren't safe yet, as they needed to head to *Parth*, do some dealing, then make it on to *Lacot*.

If such a place really existed.

Ghost towns. That was the term everybody on the ship was using now to describe it. A town all built up and then abandoned so suddenly that everything remained intact and forgotten.

All the buildings, none of the people.

Parth wasn't filled with ghosts yet, at least according to all the current details, but at the same time, news moved slowly on the Periphery. Tessa had no idea how much of what they might buy would be sellable out there. Valuable.

Save that the planning had already yielded them new contacts on *Newhall*, and even in Astoria.

Not that she wanted to go legitimate, but looking out over the street, she could see things she'd been missing in her years on the fringe.

Noise awoke her from her slumbers. Fin and the others tromping back up to the front, happily chattering and excited in ways she hadn't seen her husband do in a while.

Already, the mission was a success, and they hadn't even left.

She turned away from the town and walked over to where they were dickering, almost bantering like old friends, for all they'd known each other for ten minutes or so.

Sometimes, it worked out like that. Having Abigail along helped, because she was everybody's friend, able to put them at ease.

"Am I broke?" Tessa teased as she walked up and kissed Fin on the cheek.

"No, but if we don't sell it all, I might end up repainting a few walls on my bridge to break up the current color scheme," he grinned. "And knitting you a sweater for winter."

MacGeorge finally wrote it all down and handed her a bill of lading. Tessa nearly squawked at the final price.

"You sure you didn't leave anything out?" she asked the man.

She'd walked in here expecting to pay at least twice as much. Maybe three times.

"Most of this is here for the locals," he nodded knowingly. "Or folks who make the trip into town because I carry such goods. My usual prices have to reflect things sitting on the shelf for years in some cases. Here, I'm making a tidy profit and can send out orders to restock from the bigger worlds. If, as you noted, more folks will be living on *Newhall* instead of *Alfann*, maybe the town will grow. Or at least be generating more traffic to some of the bigger places, like *Beaumonde*. I can afford to have hardly any stock right now while I wait. And folks at *Parth* will appreciate it all. Plus, I'm certain that we'll be hiring you to carry a box with post for them."

Tessa shook her head but smiled. Dug out coins and covered it all.

"Now, let us get you loaded," the old man said.

Turned out to be almost too many boxes for the flatbed, but Tessa was able to tie everything down. As long as Fin didn't get into a car chase today.

"Until tomorrow," MacGeorge said as they loaded themselves.

"Until then," Tessa nodded.

"Thank you!" Fin called as he powered the truck up and spun it around.

Quickly, they retraced their path to the ship, with Abigail turned around.

"This feels bigger than I had expected," Abigail said, face furrowed with concern. "Are we up to something I should know about?"

"I think that we've all gotten infected with a little excitement," Tessa grinned. "Things have been a little too predictable lately."

"Predictable," Abigail said with a perfectly straight face. "Exactly what I expect from you two. The two fugitives and one refugee we've taken aboard qualify as the usual fare, yes?"

She was grinning too, but Abigail knew their business better than most.

"Something new," Fin offered. "Out of the way and off the beaten path."

Tessa agreed.

It was useful to step outside yourself every once in a

while, if only to look around. Maybe learn who you'd become, or maybe were threatening to.

Stretch yourself.

Not that she was tired of a life of crime, but a girl needed options.

Scene Seven

Tessa had supervised loading art supplies down in the cargo bay. Along with a box of mail from MacGeorge's friends. Plus the usual groceries and such you got when heading out into space. Everything was packed up. Everyone was settled in.

She headed forward and up. Found Fin on his bridge, just clearing the atmosphere and letting the blue skies fade to the blackness of space.

Rather than speak, she settled in the co-pilot seat and watched him perform that specific competence porn that got her all happy to see him. Firm hands, but delicate with touch. Just enough pressure to push buttons without going too far. Flying the entire ship from muscle memory, to the point he could do all this in the dark.

"You appear to be breathing heavy," he noted out of the corner of his eye, drawing the wheel around and back as he got out beyond the gravity of the surface.

"Just enjoying the show," she countered, verbally switching places with the man from how it normally went when she stepped out of the shower in the morning.

He grinned like a newborn star.

"Had a thought," Fin said after a few moments. "Instead of going to *Parth* first, I'd like to pivot and look for *Lacot* instead."

"Any particular reason?" she asked.

"Got a whole planet, if we're lucky," he nodded. "Like flying out of Astoria, I was surprised at how many folks there must be, for all the fields I saw regular-like as I went overhead. No true cities as such, but a long series of little villages kind of clustered along a road that mostly followed a riverbed. 'How big is Astoria?"

"Roughly twenty thousand folks if you include transients," she said. "Not the biggest place on *Newhall*, but the one best suited to our line of work."

"Wondered about that," he replied. "Easily twice that in what I saw flying past. Made me wonder what I might see from the night sky over *Lacot*. Or *Parth*."

"Planets are big places," Tessa noted. "Even thinly populated, you can pack a lot of settlers in there. Mostly it requires time to build up, since things happen on generational scales."

"Slow to grow, fast to die?" he asked.

"If something went wrong and you had to abandon a settlement, sure," she agreed. "Maybe a plague sweeps through and suddenly you don't have enough survivors to keep bloodlines from getting thin. Family trees that don't have branches because you end up with nobody to marry but a cousin. That sort of thing. A lot of times, it's easier to pick up stakes and move on. If you all left on the same ship, nobody would take the time to tear down things, especially if you thought you might go back later."

"You ever think about going back to Zaddinul?" he asked.

"Absolutely freaking not," she scowled. "They got what

they had coming. However, if you decided that you needed to go live in Inleah at some point, I might be much more amenable."

"That's good to know," her husband grinned. "Doubt that we'll face that need any time soon. Don't know if my parents actually excised me from the will, or merely threatened to. Probably won't until one of them dies, which is hopefully never, because I don't want to be a banker."

"So why has *Lacot* captured your imagination so?" Tessa asked.

She knew the man's opinions of his parents. And family. And the threats to denounce and disown him if he married *one of them.*

Not that they'd ever met Tessa. Only responded badly to the letter he'd sent indicating a new fiancée with a few pictures and inviting them to a wedding.

They hadn't come. Hadn't sent a gift.

Fin still seemed to think he got the better end of that deal. She certainly had a unicorn on her hands.

Fin's eyes had that faraway dreamer look he got.

"On *Dastow*, back in Inleah, things are quiet," he finally began. "Zorthone is a boring town, filled with bankers, accountants, actuaries, and the people who prey on them. Little gray men in pretty gray suits. Not a lot of stars in the night sky, because of the various nebulae around."

He glanced over and she nodded, having heard all this previously.

"I wanted to see those stars close up," Fin continued. "Touch them, as it were. Only child, so my parents kind of spoiled me. Probably hoping that I'd get over my fascination with flying and get back to the family business. Little gray men in pretty gray suits. Yuck, ya know?"

"Indeed I do," Tessa agreed.

"After I'd escaped their greedy, clutching claws, I met

you, and it was all over for me," he smiled, and Tessa felt warm all over, too. "So I guess what I'm trying to say is that *Lacot* is that question of what's over the next horizon, or something like that, if it makes any sense."

"Does," Tessa agreed. "I'm never going back to Zaddinul, but that's because some fool lord would decide that either I had escaped from one of his farms, or that I was a tribe that should have been wiped out in the first place. I'm personally hoping that Lorastir somehow civilizes those punks, even if they had to use a length of pipe to do it. What are you thinking we might find out there?"

She'd almost said *you* instead of *we*, but this was a joint venture. He hardly ever asked for much, so she appreciated the chance to indulge him occasionally.

"Dunno," Fin said. "Half of me never wants to go, because then it's always out there beckoning me. The other half is sitting in the back seat like Wyatt, asking if we're there yet."

Tessa laughed with her whole chest, visualizing the big man doing exactly that.

"This way," he said, "we can get there and prove that it exists. Then go on to *Parth* once we figure out what we might need. Or what they might need if we find folks on *Parth* to talk to. No clue, but *Parth* is a lot closer. And maybe folks hiding on *Lacot* will appreciate knitting patterns and tiny bottles of paint in every color under the rainbow. Assuming they don't open fire on sight."

"Assuming," Tessa agreed.

Some folks would want to hide from the rest of the universe, maybe sneaking into town so quietly that only folks like MacGeorge knew they were there. He'd be the one quietly filling their orders and not talking much to folks like her, except when Fin wandered in and was his charming, disarming self.

Man could strip you naked without ever laying hands on you. Just using his words and his eyes. Seduce you right into his bunk then convince you to stay all night.

Not that he'd ever done that to her.

"You're smiling and breathing heavy again," he said.

"Let me know when you can put things on autopilot," Tessa said rising. "I might need to remind you again why you put up with me."

They shared a grin, like they shared so much else.

And together, maybe it was time for a different kind of adventure.

Scene Eight

Tessa studied the world of *Lacot* that she could see out the forward glass, sitting next to Fin the copilot's seat. She could hear folks breathing behind her, ranging backwards in height, with Abigail having a hand on her shoulder and Wyatt all the way in back.

Planet. Pretty, but a lot more brown than most.

"That's it?" Laney asked.

It had been her map that started all this.

"That's what we find at those coordinates," Fin sort of corrected her. "As to what we might find below, I have no clue."

"Are there large bodies of water?" Wyatt asked.

Even Tessa turned to look at the big man. He blushed something fierce.

"Folks like to live on the beach," he stammered, beet red. "They put cities on the edge of the ocean when they can, usually where a big river emerges from the hinterlands to intersect. Not so necessary today, when you can just fly somewhere, but riverboats have historically been a preferred means of transportation and communication in primitive societies."

Tessa would have bet that the man didn't even know the meaning of some of those words until now. But then, he liked to play big and dumb, and you had to know him pretty well to encounter the brains underneath.

He blushed some more. Folks nodded and turned back her way.

She was still the captain around here.

She looked at Fin.

"Sure," he shrugged nonchalantly. "Let me spend a few hours in orbit, looking at my options, then we can fly down lower and see what we see."

Tessa nodded. She rose, waving everyone back and down the stairs. Fin would prefer to do this in privacy. Nobody breathing his air while he thought thinky thoughts. She was the same way, so she got them all aft and into the kitchen.

Abigail must have been reading her mind, because she put on the big pot of water, rather than the small one. Enough for tea for everyone.

There was a lot of everyones these days, and Tessa was still getting used to so many faces. Friendly, but it had been just her and Fin for a while with Auntie, before adding Wyatt. Then Abigail. Then three more wanderers.

Wyatt took a spot at the table and let his face get all grumbly. His quiet way of asking to be left alone. He'd said his intellectual piece. Might not use a two-syllable word again for a week, just to make a point.

Tessa grinned and moved to the chair at the far diagonal from the big man, giving him all the space between. The others filed in with her, but at her end.

She could practically smell the excitement around her. Folks had talked about it for days, but now they were here. Seeing something that might be magical.

Tea got made. Folks made small talk, but didn't really talk about the planet below them. They'd chewed it back and forth for a week now, and that bone was pretty clean.

Instead, they just sat and sipped tea or coffee as was their wont. Auntie, Wyatt, Abigail, Laney, Constanz, and Brianna. Relaxed and left her husband to do his thing.

Fin came back a while later. Folks hadn't done much of anything beyond smile at each other. He seemed a bit surprised to find them all present, but moved over and got some tea going for himself.

"I might have identified a couple of good candidates," he said as his tea steeped.

Tessa wasn't alone in turning to start expectantly at him. Fin grinned.

"Based on Wyatt's logic," Fin said, pausing as the big man got to blushing again, "there is an ocean. After looking at a few things, I found a few promising spots and pointed the camera at them. One looks like it has a square road grid. Late in their day now, so I propose that we adjust our clocks to drop down early morning and park in some nearby hills, driving the truck over."

"Why not fly down and land nearby?" Constanz asked.

"They might not be friendly," Tessa said. "Planet that nobody knows about, in the middle of nowhere. Might be pirates. Might just be anti-social and willing to shoot on sight. Won't know until we get there."

"Oh."

Tessa nodded at the man friendly-like. She had to think of him as a man. Identcard said *Constanz McLaren. Gender: Male.* Dressed and presented that way, too.

All a load of hooey. Constanz was the older sister and Brianna the younger, pretending to be a married couple to hide from the authorities who had big bounties on both their heads from when Constanz had broken his sister out of some sort of secret research facility.

And while he might be a brilliant surgeon, that boy hadn't been out in the real world all that much. Not like the Periphery.

Whole other galaxy out here, once you left the supposedly civilized Arles Region.

"But you did see something like roads?" Brianna asked.

Tessa turned to the other sister. Simply the most beautiful woman probably any of them had ever seen. Pretty to begin with, then plastic surgery on top of that to achieve perfection.

Supposedly smarter than her sister. Even less experience in the outer rims.

And more than a little crazy, from what those folks had done to her in their quest to create the perfect assassin.

"Something," Fin nodded. "Maybe docks, too. Hard to tell from this far up, but it gives us a starting point."

"Lights at night?" Abigail asked.

"Plan to check in a bit, as night falls on them, but I haven't seen anything significant elsewhere on the planet so far, so I don't have high hopes."

Tessa understood that. All this way and it might really be a ghost town. All those supplies they'd loaded up, but she still had *Parth* to visit, and an understanding from MacGeorge that the things they'd bought would go over well there.

If she broke even on this run, that was a win. Ships were expensive propositions.

Still, she was hoping that there was someone down on the ground to make all this adventure somehow more real in her mind.

SCENE NINE

Fin studied the horizon indicator on his console. They were coming out of the east, with the sun rising behind him. Flying into the darkness as the terminator raced away from the ship.

Anyone looking his way would be blind, and he'd seen no indications of any sort of electronic life. Not even a communications satellite above him or a weather radar on the planet below.

Might be dead. Might be playing possum.

He had a lot of experience telling lies as he flew. Thus, out of the sun. Arc around the north into a bevy of hills that were sharp enough to keep farmers and ranchers from getting up in here, particularly with so much of a nicer river valley over there to work with.

Not the first time he'd snuck in someplace low and fast at first light to hide from folks with binoculars, either.

Tessa was with him. Rest of the folks were cleaning up after breakfast and getting themselves psyched up for a new adventure. Wyatt was the only one aft with experience at this sort of thing, and Auntie had already announced that she was planning on pulling some maintenance while the ship was on the ground and nobody around.

"Is that it?" Tessa asked.

"That's the shoreline," Fin agreed. "The bay we want is about ten kilometers south of here, but I also plan to land a little inland."

He put word to deed and elevated a bit. Not much, but *Last Stand* had been practically surfing for the last few minutes, hardly more than one hundred meters in the air where things were thick and damp, and you were invisible at any distance at all.

That last one was the important part.

"Is it really that warm over there?" Tessa asked, tapping a forward sensor.

"Once you get inland, most places warm up," he nodded. "The ocean moderates things, but the air is crossing an entire continent before it gets here. So yeah, warm a lot of the time. Probably cold in the short winter they likely get at this distance from the star."

"So not a place for farmers?" Tessa pressed.

Fin shrugged.

"I know less about farming than just about anybody," he said. "I suppose you could raise livestock. If they are on that bay, maybe fishing?"

"Depends on what you find in the ocean," Tessa replied. "Things that get seeded are usually pretty standard, but they get weird in a hurry."

"Story of my life," Fin chuckled.

Then he was concentrating on flying, as the coastline swept past below him.

He'd dropped below the speed of sound while still a ways out to sea, so nobody should hear him coming unless he flew right over them at this point. Couldn't be helped then.

Scrublands below. High humidity to keep things moist,

but not a lot of rainfall, or this would look less like desert and probably more like swamp or jungle.

But then, warm planet. Pretty dry, looking from orbit. Cheap real estate, though, in a big galaxy.

Good place for someone to hide.

Fin throttled back as he went, looking for a nice place to settle, mostly out of sight but with access to the south. Someplace he could hide and drive over.

There. Flat. Open. Even a creek with a bit of water flowing, looking more like an artesian spring. He could always top off the tanks if it was clean enough.

Fin had been worried he'd have to boil away all the ocean's salt first, so this was already an improvement.

"All hands, stand by for landing," he announced. "We at Sladek/Barton Spaceways would like to thank you for flying with us today and look forward to serving your transport needs wherever your adventures in lawlessness might take you."

Tessa chuckled. Then he was deploying gear and hovering as he slewed the ass end around, looking for the best spot to set her down.

He dropped, landing like a pillow as all the feet touched and bit.

Fin powered down and turned to his badass warrior wife with a smile.

"We're here."

Scene Ten

Tessa counted noses. Auntie was remaining behind, mostly because she wasn't all that into adventure, much of the time. Tessa occasionally needed her to pick locks and deal with power systems, but they were only exploring today.

She hoped.

Wyatt was armed with *Doomripper*. She had her rifle. Laney and Brianna both had pistols they'd stolen along the way. Constanz had actually sniffed at her when Tessa suggested he be armed, bringing along his little, black bag instead.

He was a doctor. A surgeon.

Good enough. Again, she hoped they didn't need medical help on anything.

Fin was driving the truck. Abigail and Constanz were up front with him scrunched in on the bench because they both had the narrowest shoulders.

Tessa supposed that it made a certain bit of sense. The four deadliest ones were all in the bed, riding along as Fin bounced over the rough terrain.

No roads up here. Not much of anything, really. He'd originally planned on skirting the edge of the creek, but Tessa had asked her husband to take them to the top of a nearby ridge.

She wanted to see what was down there.

He pulled up and everybody got out. The valley stretched into the distance south, and almost forever inland when she turned that way. Binoculars came out and she zeroed in on the spot where the river down there connected with a bay. Or maybe widened out into a delta.

She could see various channels, plus spots where the river itself had moved around over the however many centuries.

And a town. Something. Not as long and strung out as Astoria, but it had a lot of that same feel. Looked like it ran along the riverbank, lending credence to Wyatt's theory about traffic on the water.

Closer to the water, the buildings got bigger. Or at least longer. Maybe not longer but with space between them? Blocks back from the riverfront?

She handed the glass to Wyatt and studied what she could see from here. Not much, but she'd seen what she needed.

People down there, at least at one point. Tessa hadn't seen a soul moving around, but it was early. And she was looking at the backside of town, where everyone looked to have a facing onto a road running along the river.

"And?" Fin asked.

"Town," Tessa nodded. "Might be abandoned. Might be they sleep until noon."

"Fishermen never sleep in," Laney spoke authoritatively. "Usually, they are gone at first light, if not earlier. We might have flown over some coming in."

"Didn't see anybody," Fin said. "And I was low enough I might have. If they heard us, they might have radioed as well, but I haven't heard anything from the planet that wasn't natural."

Nods.

Civilization was a noisy thing. Satellites and stations in orbit, expensive as they were to build and maintain. Radar and landing beacons on the surface. Entertainment on various radio frequencies.

Lacot, and this was the planet in question based on those old coordinates, was dead silent.

Or the silence of the dead.

Something.

Everyone got a chance to look, but nobody had anything to add.

No movement. No radio calls that Auntie would be monitoring for, back at the ship.

How long would a ghost town survive, if everybody left?

Trick question. How well had it been built? How bad was the weather? Were there any sea monsters that might come along and destroy things, like that one comic book she'd read as a kid?

They piled back into the truck and headed over the ridge. Just enough grass that Fin wasn't throwing roostertails of dirt in the air. Just enough trees that they weren't immediately visible forever if someone happened to look this way.

Fin was being careful today. The truck was electric, and therefore quiet when it rolled. Only the sound of knobby tires in the dirt as they approached. He came in from the low end of town, where they had space to maneuver if they needed it, rather than immediately being surrounded by buildings if trouble hit.

River was broad and slow. Made sense, as the terrain in this valley was flat. Water almost looked sluggish. Wide, too, with no bridges across. No roads, save what feet and maybe little trucks like this one had pounded flat at some point.

Fin pulled to a rest, just a few meters beyond the last building on the strip. If you could call it a strip. Always did in a starport, but those were different.

Weren't they?

"I would like to maybe park the truck right here," Fin said.

"What about over there?" Abigail was pointing. "That building looks half destroyed, but you ought to be able to back it in where the front wall kind of collapsed, in case we're making a mad dash getaway."

Tessa grinned. Abigail wasn't usually with them when that sort of thing happened. They'd send her off someplace safe so she had an alibi, if *Last Stand* got captured.

Still, it looked good. Tessa hopped off and walked over, the others in a line back to Fin.

Metal. Prefabbed and assembled. Whole front panel had given up and gone over backwards at some point.

Ghost town, then. That, or the population was so small that they didn't care about a building down at this end.

She turned and noted that Wyatt was standing next to one of the pillars upholding an overhanging roof. Not invisible, but some amount of cover if he started exchanging fire with someone.

Wyatt was like that. Army. Then crime.

Tessa looked inside. Empty enough that the wall had fallen flat.

Carefully, she walked out onto the panel, but if the river was this close, you wouldn't normally dig basements. No, you'd either set pilings into the ground or pour concrete that turned into a shallow box that you rested a house atop.

They'd done the latter here, so there would be a crawlspace below, but again, metal floors rather than wood. If you treated everything right, might last centuries.

How many?

Stripped to bare walls, but she could see where there had been art painted on at one point. Some of it had flaked off, leaving stains, while other murals and things had merely faded down to almost nothing.

Not even rats, but if there was nothing organic to gnaw on, they might find better places to hide, and she hadn't seen any tracks of larger animals. Probably around here somewhere, but unless they were people-sized, most would slink away from a mob like hers, and Wyatt wasn't likely to provoke anything.

He would, however, shoot a bear dead at the first growl.

One of the reasons she kept him around.

Tessa turned and emerged. South-ish facing, so the sun was on her face. Warm, and the day was like to get hot eventually.

"Safe?" Fin asked.

"Safe enough, I think," she answered. "Seems solid underfoot."

He nodded and drove close with utter delicacy, twisting out, then backing right up the front steps, onto that covered porch, and backwards into the space. One big room with a couple of closets she hadn't bothered exploring. Toilet, linens, or clothing racks, none of which she needed.

The mere location of a previously inhabited planet would be valuable to someone. Folks were always looking for ways to escape the law. Or at least the idiot governors that Ergrove liked to appoint.

Well-connected punks. Money. Sometimes pretty. Rarely brains. Frequently chosen for ruthlessness over anything.

Or the willingness to hire mean fuckers to get things done. Whatever.

Tessa led the group up the roadway now. Never cut by any sort of machine. Maybe cattle walking had laid out the road?

About seven meters wide. Tendency to meander along with the riverbank, leaving another twelve or fifteen meters over there she presumed meant flooding in the spring or something. Rich and green on the bank, quickly fading to browns once you got a hundred meters uphill.

She felt like a sheriff in one of those books she'd read, striding into town with her lever-action carbine in one hand, leading a posse of concerned citizens, some of them armed, to arrest someone.

Nobody jumped out. Nothing broke the morning stillness.

Hardly any breeze. Smell of desert lingering in the air, all dry and chalky.

First building had felt like a one-room apartment. There were a bunch just like it. Like they all came off the same production line and got shipped out here for assembly.

Someone had done this with organization. Whenever that had been.

Eventually, they reached a point that had the feel of an intersection. Maybe a path out into the wilderness on one side and down to the river the other direction.

Tessa looked at the one building here, ten up from the end, and considered what it might have been once.

"Feels like a bar," Abigail offered in the quiet.

Tessa nodded agreement and stepped to the front. Door was closed, but not locked. She turned the handle and had to jack a shoulder into it where the frame had settled, then it screeched inward as she pushed old hinges.

"If I cared, I'd oil that," Fin muttered, coming in right behind her.

The others joined her inside, Wyatt last and standing right next to the door looking out as much as in.

Joint was in and down two quick steps to a solid concrete floor. Tables with chairs upside down atop them like you did when cleaning for close. Bar down one side. Dust, but not a lot, so she had no way to guess if it had been abandoned for a year or a lifetime.

Not a bottle left, though. Folks had obviously prioritized things well when leaving.

"We know nobody has entered via that front door in some years," Constanz remarked. "Perhaps longer. Or is there a back door they might have used?"

Tessa followed the doc to an interior doorway that let on to a kitchen. Of sorts. Again, everything left behind. Industrial-grade stuff. Professional kitchen like a restaurant, rather than a couple of microwaves where you might nuke some burritos or nachos or something.

Pity she couldn't strip it all out. No place to put it on *Last Stand*, unless she sacrificed a quarter of her cargo bay.

Or started a flying taco truck that went from settlement to settlement.

She laughed.

"What?" Constanz asked.

"Most of this looks to be in good enough shape to steal," Tessa offered. "I got no place to put it or use it, though. Wondered if someone should put a kitchen in a small ship, replacing most of the cargo space. Land somewhere and open the bay to serve people hot, fresh food."

"That's actually reasonably common on *Baramunz*," Constanz noted. "Many neighborhoods have specifically designated parks where you can land and connect to power and water, with such vehicles rotating through a fairly set pattern."

"Really?" Tessa asked.

She came from a poor world. Or the poor part. The nobles had never gone hungry. Probably summoned such trucks to their palaces when they wanted to slum like common folk. When even Abigail's cooking might pale after a while and they needed something new for that latest hit of excitement in their lives.

"Truly," Constanz nodded. "I cannot see such a thing working in Astoria, though."

"You'd need to be hitting the farming communities," Fin spoke up.

He'd flipped a chair to sit and then a second one to rest his feet on. But then, he'd done all the flying and driving to this point as well, with everyone else passengers.

Tessa and Constanz both turned.

"Lots of small places beyond Astoria on *Newhall*," he nodded to them. "None of them rich enough to support a fancy restaurant, I'm guessing, but if your money got enough velocity going, you could buy fresh food from them as you went and make a nice living, flitting around from village to village like a honeybee."

Not what Tessa wanted to do with her life, but not all that far from what she was doing now. Other than she'd need to make sure she could get away and then disappear into Flightspace if the authorities ever caught up with her.

"So much lost potential," Brianna mused, standing near the bar and drawing a finger through the dust that had accumulated. "They had all this, then left."

"Many worlds out there that folks could settle on," Abigail offered. "And endemic poverty, both from the war as well as the aftermath. Settlements are expensive and fragile. This one was unable to entice sufficient population to sustain. Or suffered some cataclysm that ended it. Should we look closer to the center?"

Tessa nodded. She was the last one out and pulled the door closed behind her for reasons she couldn't even explain to herself. Other than it had remained sacrosanct for this long. No reason to be a barbarian and tear it any further down.

Folks might want to come along later and make this a place again.

Across the street, that was the bodega. The little shop where you found things. The shopkeeper who ordered them from off-world for you. MacGeorge would live here, in the small second story she could see above. Buildings were getting larger now. Taller, too. Village turning into town.

Ghost town, but still a town.

Again, stripped bare inside. Shelves and racks around the outside and interior, like rings around a central counter where the keeper would watch her stock. Dusty glass and dusty counters. Space in back for storage, but it looked like critters had gotten in at some point, because boxes and debris were scattered everywhere.

No rat droppings she could find.

They gathered again in the street, river on their right, buildings on their left. Wilderness behind them, town growing more complicated ahead.

"So which one of these would you build as the city hall?" Tessa asked the group.

"Do we suppose they did organized religion?" Fin asked.

Everyone turned to look at him in unison.

"Back home, a good chunk of the population are god-bothered," he said with a shrug. "Tend to build fancy churches, so that their chief deity is impressed with the noise of their piety. Or something like that. Priests dress expensive. Live in fancy houses with lots of staff. Not exactly what their prophet suggested, but I always got the impression that most of them only skimmed large chunks of their holy book. Still, if we presume, then the city hall would be the second nicest building. Otherwise, it might be first. One of those three, anyway."

He was pointing. Tessa grunted and started walking.

Fin had been raised in Inleah. Folks had stayed out of the

war, neutral and mercenary. She supposed that they might feel the need for some god to forgive them for all the things they did or sold in the process of helping Lorastir conquer Altenfeld and then Zaddinul.

And whoever might be next.

Might be Ergrove. Might not. Lorastir had enormous land armies to maintain occupations, but not a lot of warships. Ergrove had a huge fleet and a willingness to blockade or bombard planets that pissed them off. Kept their settlement worlds in Hawkswold Sector compliant. And other Periphery Sectors like Boystone, Erley, Waywood, Owlsdale, or Cewich.

Behave or be punished.

They trod into town.

"Hey," Laney called suddenly. "Everybody stop moving."

Tessa had her rifle up and covering the front, just as Wyatt would have the city-side flank.

"What?" she called without looking back.

"At your feet," Laney said. "Tracks."

Tracks?

Tessa looked down and blinked hard. Shit, those were footprints. People, even.

What the hell were they doing here?

SCENE ELEVEN

Laney didn't like to call up the old memories. Buried was a good place for them. She was always surprised that she hadn't been buried with them.

Sometimes, they bubbled to the surface, and she had to deal with them.

Like now.

Tracks. Evidence of humans walking around, and not just large animals. Not like bears. They had a specific spoor, as did most things.

Lots of worlds out there that had been terraformed in some distant past, but nobody really knew when. Or by whom, but there had been an apocalyptic interlude along the way that made the bloody Lorastir revolution of her youth look like a picnic softball game by comparison.

Laney moved up next to Captain Sladek and knelt. Boot marks. Modern. Cheap, because they'd hired a cobbler to resole their boots, but hired an amateur. Or a drunk. Asymmetric, not as a fashion statement. Smooth, though.

She studied the print.

The soil around here was usually damp, but it felt like the dry season on this world. Or at least this part. Not fresh, which was really her first worry.

Someone had walked here after enough rain that the roadway itself had gotten a little slushy. Stepped just so and sank enough to leave a mark, but only the one, before getting back onto the hardpan.

Then the sun had come out and everything had dried in place.

Little weathering, so less than a few months, depending on climate conditions she didn't know. Older than a week.

She looked up at the anxious faces.

"Recent, but not that recent," she pronounced. "Maybe a month."

She watched the Captain's face go through the usual calculations you got with someone in charge. Weighing odds and options.

Laney had never been an officer, except on paper. To give her a uniform she could wear when the brass insisted on it because seeing someone in civilian attire inside their headquarters offended them.

Bright, shiny peacocks, the lot of them. Noisy and annoying.

Laney had kept such visits as rare and short as possible.

But she knew commanders. Tessa Sladek-Barton was a good one.

"Do we know how many people there are?" she asked. "Or were?"

Laney looked down. One male, from the size. Tall but not that heavy. Walking that direction.

Laney rose and moved forward slowly, eyes down but the pistol she'd brought with her in hand now, though she couldn't remember drawing it.

Some things got to be automatic after a while. Like those old memories and old skills that wouldn't stay buried.

She supposed that her nightmares would again be especially vivid for a while.

Fool had been walking on damp ground. And staying off to one side, right along the verge with the grass, which made no sense.

Unless the roadway was packed so well that it turned into a lake in the rainy season.

Laney could see folks not taking the time to trench, gravel, sand, and slope a roadway properly for drainage. Took a lot of work. And you tended to make your roads straight when you did it that way.

Cattle trail.

"One person on this trail," Laney said. She couldn't help it that her voice fell to a whisper. In her mind, she was stalking a target again. Something she'd been doing since the Captain was in diapers. "Headed inward along the path we were following, but staying off the road itself and squelching through mud. Again, not that recent. Maybe a month."

"A month is recent enough," Sladek growled quietly. "Do we presume they heard or saw us approaching today and all went to hide?"

"That is an option, Captain," Laney said. "At that point, do we wish to confront them?"

"Got no reason for that," Sladek said. "If they don't want company, foisting ourselves on them won't improve their humor."

"They might think we're pirates," Brianna opined.

"We aren't exactly that far off, when you get right down to it, McLaren," Tessa replied. "At least from their perspective."

"I did not see any ships when I was looking from orbit," Fin spoke up from near the back. "Nor when I was on final approach. I still hid *Last Stand*, but there's no place to conceal something that size around here. Not unless one of these buildings retracts the roof sideways to reveal some giant, underground base. You know, like in that one movie."

Laney had no idea what they were talking about, but she knew those two had a second language that they shared, impenetrable to an outsider.

"Nothing recent?" Sladek asked Laney.

"Nothing recent," Laney agreed. "Should I continue or did you wish to withdraw?"

Indecision. Not executive paralysis, *per se*, but being forced to guess the best of a set of bad options. Officer stuff.

Laney understood that she could have been a real officer. Just as Wyatt might have. Neither of them would have been happy. She had spotted the man enough while weightlifting by now to have a better feel for him.

Wyatt was always playing possum.

"Hey, is that a ship?" Wyatt suddenly barked.

Laney spun in place to see where the man was pointing. A dot on the western horizon.

"Everybody off the street **now**!" Fin Barton yelled sharply.

Bodies slid across the road and under an overhanging porch.

There was a boom, low and sharp.

Starship, dropping below the speed of sound, whatever it was on this planet.

Final approach? Awfully fast.

Almost as fast as Laney used to do it, when she was on a Lorastir privateer hunting Zaddinul renegades. Not that she spoke of those days in anything but the vaguest terms.

Captain Sladek didn't need Laney's history causing her trouble. Nor did the McLarens.

Laney really wanted to vanish from history at this point.

Recover from the life of a secret agent. Living a lifetime of killing and lying all the time.

She was retired now. And tired.

And, it seemed, only accidentally a criminal and pirate by association.

Still, something of a step up from the old days.

"Fin, where would you land?" Sladek asked her husband as everyone got out of sight.

"We're basically on the two-seventy approach," the pilot said, referencing *west*. "There was a spot about three-twenty, where the bay starts to bell out. Open spot that I took for a park or athletic pitch from above. Might also be a landing field."

So, northwest. Close to the center of town and the presumed city hall. Back from both the river and the harbor. Dry land, whereas a ship might be too heavy and would sink, closer to the water, unless there was a lot of granite underfoot.

Laney turned to Captain Sladek, both of them automatically counting noses around them. Everyone accounted for. Not all of them ready for a life of piracy, though at this point Laney supposed that even Constanz McLaren had proven to be tougher than Laney had originally given the doctor credit for.

"Captain, we should, at a minimum, withdraw to safety," Laney said.

"Agreed," Sladek said. "Let's get them on the ground first, then we'll immediately move to that bar we found. The front door will open if we move it quietly, then we hide inside and watch to see if they saw us or *Last Stand*."

"Should we not flee entirely?" Laney asked.

"We're on wheels, Laney," the Captain replied. "They're flying. They can outrun us, and if they do come in and land here, then likely they didn't see our ship. I don't want to lead them there if they can get there first."

"Oh," Laney nodded.

She had to agree with the logic. Sneakiness was called for. Possibly extreme violence later.

This group was certainly well-prepared for both.

Overhead, the whine of ship's engines rose in volume.

Scene Twelve

Fin listened as the other ship came in. They were in the middle of nowhere, in a space where there weren't any folks around.

Except, he amended himself, that local folks might have known that they had friends coming and chosen to hide. That would suggest women and children, with the menfolk racing madly back from somewhere.

Not good.

Tessa had gotten the bar door open quickly, gotten them all in, then closed it again. He'd gone through the kitchen door on Wyatt's heels, with Laney right behind him, to the back door. Constanz was along with them, but mostly staying back and watching, like he did.

The door back there had been bolted from the inside. Fin couldn't move the bar.

"Wyatt, I might have a jar of pickles here," Fin told the big guy.

Half the reason he kept Wyatt around. Opening pickle jars and retrieving things from high shelves.

Didn't much help that Abigail was the only one here shorter than him.

Wyatt grunted a generic profanity under his breath and handed Fin *Doomripper*. Fin held it like a newborn as the big guy got under the bar and straightened. Rust, sure, but mostly the building settling and flexing the door frame a shade.

About like opening a jar of pickles.

Fin nodded and the man pulled it open as well. Stiff, but that would mean it held when some fool tried to put a boot into it later if they'd been seen.

Fin stuck his ear to the gap and listened. The ship was on final approach now, riding thrusters.

One of them was falling out of alignment with the other three from the tone, but he didn't know if that was a repair issue or a bad pilot not keeping his collective balanced.

You could tell a lot about a pilot and crew merely by listening to them land.

Folks over there really weren't overwhelming him with their competence at this point.

Roar went off the charts right then, but that was them flying overhead rather than hovering to drop killers, like he occasionally did with Tessa and Wyatt when they were breaking into a robot-piloted moving vehicle.

Fin looked up. By size, he'd say top end of *Snekka*, rather than the larger *Skeid*. Thanks to whichever gods were watching out for him that it wasn't a *Drakkar*. Last thing he needed right now was a dragonship. Granted, the name Skeid literally meant *fast* in some ancient language that modern folks had inherited. Snekka was still a warship, but smaller. More than enough folks to vastly outnumber his crew, if they were anything at all, though.

He looked at his two cohorts.

"You can get this closed in a hurry if I need it?" he asked.

"Piece of cake," Wyatt nodded. "Might not seal to rain, but I can wedge the bar in place and they'll be better off trying to come through a window at that point."

Fin nodded. Only windows in the kitchen were high up for light, rather than letting folks look in. You'd have to be on somebody's shoulders or coming off the roof of a tall land vehicle to get in.

And shit would have gone much farther sideways.

"Keep watch," he told them. "Listen, but keep the door open for now."

They nodded and he went up front to find Tessa and Brianna ducked behind the bar with Abigail. Invisible from outside, and that bar looked like it would stop anything that didn't require a tripod to shoot.

He slipped in.

"Medium-sized ship," Fin told her. "Probably a heavy Snekka, so fully loaded you're looking at about three dozen gunmen. Enough to be a pain in the ass to anybody. They've landed, but didn't seem like a combat drop to me. More like *sliding in, glad to be home, and who's fixing dinner?* kind of thing. Got the back open to listen, but Wyatt can close it up after shooting a few folks if he needs to."

"Because heaven forbid Wyatt not be able to shoot someone," Tessa rolled her eyes.

He grinned.

"Plan, beautiful?" he asked.

"Wait here for now," she said. "If they want to surround us, we've got steel and concrete for protection, so either they storm the place in the face of massive casualties, or back off. Hoping they were too lazy to even notice we were there."

"Just glad Abigail suggested parking the truck inside," Fin grinned at the tiny woman. "Doubt they make it down there all that often. At least until they have a reason."

Tessa stood at this point. Or sort of stood. Up and bent

over the bar with her chin on her hands in a most distracting way, as it stuck her bottom out. He considered a quick caress, but the situation probably didn't justify it.

Probably.

So he and the other two women popped up and watched. If you weren't standing with your nose against the dirty glass, the southern sun probably hid the interior entirely, but you didn't want movement drawing the eye.

"How long do we wait?" Brianna asked.

"If they were coming, they'll come quick," Tessa told the woman. "Get us surrounded and pinned."

"Do we assume that there were folks around, and they called for help?" Fin asked.

"Possibility," Tessa glanced over. "At the same time, we saw no evidence of folks around."

"So we might have been a few hours ahead of them, and came out of the east instead of gliding down with them from the west?" Fin asked.

Tessa shrugged. Nobody knew. At least until they had a local to ask.

Chances of somebody else just happening to discover this world at the exact same time were functionally impossible, unless someone had deliberately seeded that map at Astoria to draw in…tourists was the wrong term.

Victims?

Play a game like a trapdoor spider, by letting the prey come to you?

Mean thing to do. If that was the case, he might have nasty words for MacGeorge or someone when they got back to *Newhall*. Impolite, even.

He studied the sun across the river. They'd come in just after dawn. Drove down leisurely, then been exploring without any great alacrity, so it was close to local noon now.

Summer-ish, he thought, so a whole bunch of sunlight left in this day.

With nothing better to do, he headed aft.

"What are you up to?" Tessa asked as he slipped away.

"Want to see if anything in the kitchen still works," he said.

It would sure beat waiting.

Scene Thirteen

Tessa watched the street for movement. After a time, she moved from behind the heavy bar and to a spot where she had a good obtuse angle through the dirty front glass. Still nothing. And anybody coming that way really had no cover at all.

Plus, Wyatt was all set to open fire at any provocation. Ergo, silence meant he hadn't seen anybody out the back.

She turned to Abigail and Brianna. Two of the most beautiful women she'd ever seen, but about as far apart mentally as you could get. Abigail was a Player. A hired hand you paid good coin for, to come in and entertain, cook, or maybe fornicate with, though Tessa knew that not that many of the woman's customers ever involved nudity.

Not counting that one fellow who just wanted to draw or paint her.

Brianna was more beautiful, but it was all artificial. Plastic surgery by an expert working towards a template of perfection. Almost got there, too. It was the woman inside who didn't match.

Brianna was as cold and quiet as Abigail was warm and friendly. Polar opposites.

"What should we do, Captain?" Brianna asked, still a little formal around the crew.

"I'd like to scout," Tessa said. "See if they did notice us, or not. If we can sneak away, or are expecting to shoot our way out and need to call Auntie to come get us, where we can cover her with gunfire if we have to."

"Send me," Brianna replied simply.

Tessa felt her eyebrows climb up her forehead.

"Not Laney?" Tessa asked, mostly to place the woman on a scale.

"I'm as good as Laney," Brianna stated in a voice devoid of emotion.

She did that when she got emotional inside. Retreated into her head. Tessa had seen it a few times.

"As deadly?" Tessa pressed.

"More," Brianna said with a grimace. "Where she was thirty years ago physically."

"Dangerous to go alone," Tessa countered. "Should I send two people?"

"Three times as noisy, Captain," the woman shook her head. "One person can get close and get out. We don't need to steal anything from them. Just find out what they know."

"You certain?" Tessa asked.

"You don't have to do this, Brianna," Abigail interjected. "You can let Nataliya fade into memory and fully become this new person."

Nataliya. The fugitive Nataliya Horowitz, along with her sister Presley, currently hiding as her husband, Constanz McLaren, to throw off seekers. The woman had been recruited by somebody, brainwashed—or maybe wiped—and turned into a killer, supposedly. An assassin.

Tessa had seen Brianna practice various martial arts forms

in the cargo bay. Usually late at night when the woman couldn't sleep.

Deadly.

Brianna turned to Abigail.

"I don't know who I am, Abigail," she said. "I look in the mirror and a stranger looks back. I hardly even remember that other woman. The one I was when I was fourteen. But the Captain has a need, and I don't think anybody here is as good as I am at serving it. Thus, I should go."

Tessa wanted to argue. At the same time, she wanted to know just how good—how deadly—Brianna McLaren really was. She'd only heard stories up to now.

She nodded when Brianna turned back this way. Maybe it was for the best.

"Abigail, you keep watch here and yell if you see anybody," Tessa said. "I'll be right back."

She nodded Brianna into the kitchen, then followed.

As much as she wanted to do this herself, Tessa was woman enough to admit that she had at least three people here better than her.

Best to make use of them.

Scene Fourteen

Brianna—she had to consciously think of herself with that name, else the nightmares would surface during the day—stood at the back door to the kitchen. Wyatt Nakada and Laney Coburn watched her with indifferent eyes that didn't hide their doubt.

Fin Barton simply smiled encouragingly at her. He was like that. Utterly devoted to Captain Sladek, and thus not a threat, emotionally or physically. Nakada might want to be a threat, but she saw the reserve in his eyes.

He'd merely strip her naked with his gaze, but never so much as reach a hand in her direction without a verbal invitation. Why, Brianna wasn't sure, but Captain Sladek had the man behaving in ways most men never learned.

She turned to Sladek now.

"You've got a firearm and a pocket of ammunition," the Captain said with a nod, referring to the revolver she'd taken from a man on *Newhall*. "First sound of trouble will be gunfire, so we'll come running to kill anybody giving you problems."

Brianna opened her mouth to object and got no further.

"You're part of my crew, McLaren," Tessa Sladek interrupted firmly. "We don't leave folks behind. I'd come for Wyatt. He'd come for me. We'll come for you."

Brianna closed her mouth before she said something stupid and nodded. She drew a breath deep and turned her attention to the door. It was open enough to hear a breeze outside. To smell cleaner air because the inside was cooped up and had been sealed for a long time.

Stale. Almost chewy.

Outside, the wind was coming from land, so it carried dried grass and pollen. Took her to another place, but she didn't know the name. It was from before. From the child Nataliya. Presley might remember, but they'd agreed to hardly ever talk about that past.

Maybe that had been a mistake? Would she lose the child she'd been before, if they didn't actively talk about those days? Presley had already been away at college, being brilliant, so she had gaps her sister wouldn't know, but they could go back deeper in time.

She turned to her sister, looking at the impostor in the male suit. Constanz McLaren, pretending to be her husband because the authorities were looking for a pair of women on the run, instead of newlyweds. It had even worked.

Presley was several steps away, but nodded to her and smiled. They would have to rethink everything, because until this moment, Brianna hadn't really understood that Tessa Sladek had accepted them, reward money and all, as crew. As family.

Even Laney Coburn nodded. She was the most like this new person Nataliya had been turned into. The one hiding as Brianna. Killers, both of them. Laney had three decades experience. Brianna had better knees and back.

One more quick breath and a smile to all the folks believing in her. Upholding her.

Brianna chose to slip out the back door and let the breeze engulf her.

On her left, something of a back yard, where there were no trees and the ground had been pounded flat at some point. On the right, the street out front turned into a second block that ran to the center of town. Housing over there, like that first, tiny space where Finlay Barton—*Fin, just Fin*—had left his transport. Buildings where the settlement could grow, turning into shops and offices once it got big enough.

She wondered idly if it ever had. And how long that had lasted.

At least she was dressed for something like this, in a pleated skirt that came to mid-calf. A brown that wouldn't show dust or dirt, and gave her space to move suddenly if she needed to.

Back in the Arles Region, Empire waists and pencil skirts were a thing, limiting women physically in ways that Brianna found terribly offensive.

But those people supported that crass psychopathic social climber as emperor, so they had largely brought it on themselves.

Under her lightweight brown jacket she had picked a white linen shirt, with two layers underneath to obscure everything while still breathing in the expected heat. Wasn't broiling yet, but she could smell that in the air as well. Soon.

Sensible boots with a low, walking heel, when ladies were often expected to have a ten to sixteen centimeter spike for height. And to be walking on polished marble floors.

Footwear alone told the biggest tale of the differences between *Lacot* and the Imperial Capital at *Falorea*.

Brianna absorbed the smells and sights, then slid to the near corner, turning all directions, but seeing nothing.

She paused, then walked across the street like a pedestrian. That had been pounded into her at the…*academy*. Furtive people looked furtive, and drew the eye. Casual deflected attention. Slid it off like water from a duck.

Brianna concentrated on *casual*. Across the street, where there was a narrow alley that both sides let onto. Too narrow for anything larger than Fin's transport, but you could always make deliveries via the front door.

The locals hadn't been planning for how the town could turn into a metropolis, save that this center might be all torn down in some future generation and turned into a park or something.

Or abandoned to the wilderness entirely.

Or pirates.

Brianna focused on her heart rate, keeping it slightly elevated but controlled. Ready for action, which might involve a sudden punch, running away, or opening fire. Except that doing so would draw the others into trouble.

She would use her fists and feet until she had no choice. Better she die alone than everyone go down with her.

Fin had pointed the way. She followed his architectural logic, creeping slowly between buildings as she got closer.

Music was the first clue that she wasn't alone. High and thin, but that might be the attenuation of distance and intervening buildings. Still, it narrowed her options.

She paused at what her mind thought of as the last corner, then oozed one eye around enough to see.

The ship was parked in an open field. She was not an expert on starships, but it gave off the impression of dinginess and age. Something that should have been retired and scrapped already. Or hauled into a yard for a major overhaul.

Barely hanging on today.

It was long and slender, like a knife balanced on the blade, instead of lying flat. Two decks that ran the whole length. Perhaps seventy meters from bow to stern, with a cargo ramp at the mouth instead of aft, like *Last Stand* did it. Bigger engine pods.

The music was coming from a nearby doorway. Or rather, someone had a phonograph sitting in the shade, playing what looked like a vinyl record up through a bell speaker. Entirely mechanical, which was much more common on the Periphery than electronics that broke down quickly.

A waltz played, drawing her mind back to classes in deportment as a youngster, learning to curtsy and dance while wearing a full gown.

Brianna shook her head and came back to the present. The song ended and voices inside the doorway became obvious. Men for the most part. Rowdy, if she had to give it an emotion.

What was it Fin had said about home and relaxing? Sailors back in port and tired of the cramped ship? Ready to drink and celebrate, then sleep in a room instead of a bunk?

The town had enough space for everyone to have their own building, let alone rooms, but she'd seen no signs of habitation anywhere but the one currently lit up next to the ship. Likely, that building was a hotel or something similar. It had that feel, now that she looked closer. Three stories tall, but long and low, with balconies on the upper floors.

A man appeared at the door, emerging into sunlight and shading his eyes from light blindness.

Brianna watched him move to the phonograph and delicately swap disks. He wound the key a few times, then stood there as music again filled the air, before heading inside.

She nodded and started to backtrack. There was a spot she should be able to get to the back of the ship and get Fin better details. It was nearly impossible to see into the nearby building without leaving cover, but she could hear many voices. Too many. Laughter, certainly, but mostly men.

All men? Hard to tell. No shrieks of rage or pain from a female mouth that she could identify. No victims being tortured or raped.

Sailors come home.

Still, pirates? The man who had been changing records had been armed. A revolver similar to hers on his hip, which you didn't need in polite company.

Therefore, impolite company. That suggested bad men. Too many to risk a confrontation.

And she was only here to scout, not kill anyone, Brianna had to remind herself. To override those voices in the back of her head that expected to be told a name and a face that needed to die. To need to turn herself into an infiltrator designed by someone else to slip in and execute a target.

Nobody knew the code words to activate her. She hoped.

Brianna withdrew. Circled back and crossed where the ship would block lines of sight.

Nobody moving around. Big engine pods facing her, with the ship resting on the ground. She got close enough to touch the hull but didn't because it might still be hot enough to sear skin. Instead, she memorized details, expecting that Fin would ask later.

Music continued to play, then paused. She peeked out from here as a different man emerged and changed records. The noise from the building beyond had redoubled, so perhaps they were winding up emotionally for a party?

Terrible time to be interrupted, as all the energy would sour quickly, looking for victims. Mobs were like that.

Idly, Brianna wondered if she could slip aboard the ship to sabotage it somehow, but feared that, like *Last Stand*, there might be mechanics still aboard fixing things. Similarly, stealing the ship would require a concerted effort of her team, but could be done.

How locked were things? Dare she attempt?

No, that way lay folly.

She waited until the man went indoors again and slipped back the way she'd come.

Scouting. Nothing more.

Nobody had seen her. Or they'd made no sign, which wasn't the same thing.

Captain Sladek needed to know.

SCENE FIFTEEN

Tessa listened to the woman's story. Almost read like a military report as she spoke, but Tessa chalked that up to the terrible things those people had done to a teenage girl. Tessa had no intention of going looking for them, but if she ever met one of the people who'd done that to Brianna, hell wouldn't save them from her.

"How many landing gear legs, again?" Fin asked.

"Eight," Brianna said. "Dual quads fore and aft, with a long stretch in the middle that had a flat bottom about a meter and a half off the ground the way they landed it."

She turned to her husband.

"Important?" Tessa asked.

"Maybe nothing," he shrugged. "Sounds like a small Skeid, rather than a large Snekka. Important because the latter is an armed cargo ship, while the former tends towards purpose-built raider crammed full of people for shorter voyages. Her theory about everybody wanting their own beds makes more sense if they were all stuffed into a Skeid and just got back from attacking someone somewhere."

"Should we do something?" Brianna asked.

Wyatt perked right up, but that was Wyatt.

"Not much we can do here," Tessa shook her head. "Got nothing but suppositions and theories at this point. No evidence of crimes. Plus, the law runs thin out here. Nobody to enforce it, and we're certainly not the good guys by any stretch of the imagination."

"Plus, if we did do something, the smartest move would be to steal their ship," Fin said. "At which point they're stranded here possibly forever, unless you wanted to tell everyone about this world. Do we?"

"What are our options?" Constanz finally broke his silence. "Obviously, they know about *Lacot* as well, so Wyatt's ghost town isn't really. Or rather, the ghosts are all likely bad men causing problems for others. Back home, we'd call them pirates."

"Do you want the authorities taking a closer look at what we're doing and who we are?" Tessa challenged. "Seems to me that would be a bad outcome all around."

After all, she had crimes that could get her thrown in jail, while Constanz and Brianna were wanted by someone bad enough to put up a huge bounty for their capture.

Constanz subsided when that idea got through.

"We do nothing," Wyatt said abruptly. "Or we do everything. I'm not seeing a lot of middle ground on this one. Personally, I vote for leaving. We can always tell somebody else about this place. Somebody with a badge and a lot of deputies who might be willing to do something about it."

"Would they, though?" Laney asked. "Each system is its own authority. I could see something like this having to go all the way to the King's government back in *Linden*. This is an Ergrove Sector, after all. They claim all these worlds, more or less."

"Hell, they might be trading with these folks already,"

Tessa offered. "Like with us, crime requires a fence. Piracy requires a bigger one, because then you need someone to keep Ergrove squadrons from chasing after you with guns and troops. Brianna, could you estimate those two men by ethnicity?"

Everyone turned to the scout. The beautiful killer in their midst.

"Ethnically Ergrove, or maybe Lorastir," she said, eyes on a horizon. "Not as dark as Zaddinul, to say nothing of you and Auntie, I'm sorry."

"Don't be," Tessa told her. "That probably means Ergrove adventurers, off doing something. As we didn't see any signs of life before they got here, and nobody come looking for us, I'm guessing that they use this as a bolt hole. A place to bring their booty and hide it while things cool down, before they haul it off somewhere and fence it. *Parth* is close, but not that big, unless you set down in the middle of some ranch and met another ship there. *Bernadette* and *Beaumonde* are both reasonably advanced, but again, you might want to keep a lower profile. Don't remember anybody like that operating out of *Alfann* or *Newhall*, but we haven't been in Astoria that long to meet everyone."

"I'm hearing a lot of *Not our fight* going around," Wyatt opined. "In that case, sun will be setting in a few hours. If nobody comes looking for us, then we should get gone. Maybe we come back at some point when they aren't here and see if we can find all their buried treasure?"

Tessa nodded. The man was big, mean, and deadly, but as he'd noted, he'd survived the war by being too smart to let them make him an officer. To have to lead troops.

Tessa was also pretty sure he'd fragged a couple of his own officers at some point.

"Sneaky is good," Tessa agreed, looking around at the others.

"I have an alternative," Abigail suddenly spoke up for the first time in a while, grinning like an evil pixie when Tessa turned to the woman. "As you know, I interact with all levels of society in my work. If I asked a few pointed questions to someone, perhaps offered hints and clues, would you be interested in me lighting the sort of fire that sends other pirates out here to maybe engage in a small war over this planet?"

Tessa forgot, occasionally, how utterly ruthless Abigail could be. At the same time, she never attached names to rumors. Ever. You might get the details, but never an attribution.

"It has legs, that idea," Tessa agreed. "At the same time, I like Wyatt's idea of maybe robbing some pirates by slipping in after they go elsewhere for supplies, and only then telling a settlement company about a place already in reasonable working order, as long as they bring a lot of guns and gunmen with them to take it over. Kinda erases all the evidence that we were involved and makes those pirates angry at someone else. And all this assumes that they were pirates. Could be any number of reasons they are here."

"Oh, sure," Fin announced in a big voice, playing along sarcastically with the occasional eye roll. "*Back to Nature Men's Movement.* Build yourself a clubhouse in the wilderness and retire from all the womenfolk for a long vacation of doing manly things, like not bathing and eating frozen pizza for breakfast."

Tessa chuckled with everyone else. He and Wyatt were surrounded by six women these days. With her in charge of things and Fin happily kept. Wyatt, for all his grumbling, didn't seem to mind her making decisions, either.

Everyone sobered and turned to her.

"We keep watch," Tessa said. "Be ready to shoot. Be ready to run. Be ready to call Auntie and let her know we need a pickup somewhere along the way if it comes to that. She's nowhere near as good a pilot as Fin, but can at least move the ship close, landing it so he can get in and start flying while we keep shooting."

"Brianna, did you see any guns or anything on the Skeid?" Fin asked.

"Guns?"

"Turret or something sticking out, like a pimple on the lower hull with a long hair growing out of it," Fin said. "Most ships are unarmed, except for warships that the authorities legally keep for themselves. If these are real pirates, they might have a gun to threaten or damage another ship, or maybe a settlement as they hover overhead."

Tessa watched the woman replay her entire penetration in memory at high speed.

"There was a beast of some sort painted on the front," Brianna said warily. "But the bow was square, as was the bottom. I didn't see the top to tell."

"You'd mount it forward or under," Fin agreed. "Pain in the ass overhead, as well as useless threatening a city. I'm willing to assume at this point that they don't have any guns, same as us. Tessa, when you sell the coordinates to someone, you should suggest they invest in some sort of ground-to-air defense battery, specifically for pirate raids like these folks might dabble in. Usually, you mount them up on a building, where you can also depress the barrel enough to shoot things on the ground. Not that I've ever had to consider such things."

Tessa rolled her eyes. They didn't attack armed settlements. Hell, the worst they ever did was to occasionally rob banks. Usually more like looting wrecks or places like this where there might be valuable surprises left behind.

Still, she nodded. They would assemble enough information to make sure someone stealing this planet was capable of holding it afterwards. She was almost tempted to ask Bao Li if that woman knew any history, but even the asking would trigger folks to ask too many questions back. And not the right ones.

"Watch and wait," Tessa reiterated. "We'll slip out when the sun gets long, if they haven't stumbled onto us by that point, then we run like hell for the ship and hope that Auntie has done nothing more than tweak generators and rebalance systems with her day. Questions?"

Nobody had any, so she nodded and let them sort themselves out. She went into the front room with Abigail and the McLarens trailing, leaving Fin in the kitchen with Wyatt and Laney.

Hopefully, nothing at all would come up today.

Scene Sixteen

Fin watched the shadows lengthen as the afternoon faded. Noise from the pirates, if you listened hard enough and the breeze was just right, but nothing more than snatches of music from that phonograph Brianna had seen earlier.

Wyatt, Laney, and Brianna had all taken quick jaunts out and around to make sure nobody was sneaking up on the group, and seen nothing. Fin had hung out and studied the hardware of the kitchen. No fuel for the generator or the stove, but otherwise they seemed to be in perfect working order.

Folks just walked away one day and never came back.

"Ghosts," he murmured to himself.

"What was that?" Wyatt asked from nearby.

"Ghosts," Fin repeated louder.

Not loud, because the back door was open and folks watching, but enough to call it a conversation.

"What about 'em?" Wyatt countered. "Ain't seen none. Unless you count us."

Fin stopped like someone had whomped him upside the head with a half-rotted sand shark.

"Shit," he grinned. "That's it."

"What's it?" Wyatt asked, turning back from the outside to glance over at Fin.

"You stay here and shoot things, big guy," Fin assured him. "Gotta talk to the boss."

Fin was having a hard time not cackling maniacally as he made his way to the front of the restaurant, heads snapping around and guns coming up.

"No, nothing," he said, hands up. "Had an idea so crazy that you might question why you married me."

"I do that already," Tessa grinned. "Or were you thinking I should trade you in on a more boring model?"

"Are there such creatures?" he asked earnestly, almost able to keep a straight face as he did.

All the folks up here laughed. He was generally quiet when he wasn't flying. Hadn't had a chance to go shopping for any new train cars for his set since they'd gone to Astoria, nor made connections. And with the things going around here, he'd put everything in storage boxes for now.

Model trains and piracy didn't always make sense to most folks. Nor was he willing to explain it to strangers.

Course, they weren't much strangers anymore, so maybe he'd pull out tracks and buildings and take over part of the cargo bay again at some point.

Anyway. Tessa was glaring at him while he gathered wool.

"Ghosts," he said emphatically.

"Ain't none," Tessa agreed with Wyatt.

"Maybe," he replied, stretching the word out to a dozen syllables as he did. "What about us?"

"Us?" Tessa asked.

"This is a ghost town," Fin said, gesturing with both hands. "Them pirates found it, likely same as we did. Kept it to themselves, but don't actually live here so much as use it like a warehouse. Can we be ghosts?"

All the folks stared, mouths wide open and eyes squinty with confusion.

Usually, a good sign.

Usually.

"What would they think if something happened in the dead of night?" Fin asked. "Nothing bad, mind you. Not an attack or crap like that. Nor stealing their ship and maybe marooning them here forever. Something small. Something delicate, even. Like ghosts playing tricks on them."

"What evil did you have in mind this time, Fin?" Abigail asked, eyes twinkling,

That woman had a deep and abiding expertise at practical jokes. Like him, she kept it under wraps when *Last Stand* was hauling passengers. But honestly, weren't the McLarens and Laney turning into crew at this point? Maybe time for everyone to let their hair down?

"Brianna saw a phonograph playing outside the ship next to the door," Fin said. "I can still hear it occasionally when the wind is just right, so somebody is winding it and swapping disks regularly. If we assume that they've been partying all afternoon, mightn't we also assume that they might be a little drunk at this point? Maybe not entirely operating plumb and level, as it were? Horizons drifting and all that?"

"With you so far," Tessa prompted.

Boss. Den mother, occasionally, but boss.

"What if we snuck in, stole the phonograph, and did nothing else?" Fin said. "At all. What would that do to them pirates if they thought that maybe the planet wasn't as abandoned as they thought? Like, maybe, just *maybe*, ghosts were watching?"

"That's rude, husband," Tessa grinned. "Most sailors are

already a mite superstitious. That might be enough to cause a ruckus."

"My thoughts exactly," Fin grinned back. "Maybe they abandon the planet entirely, if that bug gets into their mind and starts rattling about. Ghost towns. Ghosts. Bad *juju*."

Tessa turned to the resident expert. Brianna had been over there, after all.

"Can it be done?" she asked the woman.

Fin nodded and kept his mouth shut. The boss hadn't shot the idea down, so maybe it wasn't as crazy as all that. Doable was a *WHOLE*'nother story.

Brianna had this thing where she seemed to step back inside her head when she got to thinking deep thoughts. Like closing up shop and heading upstairs for tea, except in her mind. Eyes unfocused. Shoulders slumped a little. Whole body seemed to sag a little.

"Yes," she said, suddenly back and grinning like a hungry sea beast.

"Could you?" Tessa asked the woman.

Not something Fin was qualified to do. He was just the criminal mastermind this time, rather than the pilot. Helped when there was nothing to fly.

"Yes," Brianna said, simple as that.

But then, nobody *really* knew what they'd done to her, other than dangerous folk like Wyatt and Laney Coburn respected Brianna McLaren's deadliness.

Said a lot.

"However," Brianna paused.

Fin grumbled. Shame, really. He'd been looking forward to being a ghost. At least in somebody's mind.

"I will need help pulling it off correctly, if you really want ghosts," Brianna said, eyes almost as evil as Abigail's.

"What kind of help?" Tessa asked.

"I will need someone to watch my back on the stalk," Brianna replied. "They'll stay out of sight, but might need to carry the phonograph itself."

"Why?" Tessa asked. "What am I missing?"

When Brianna told them, Fin burst out laughing.

Scene Seventeen

Brianna had considered all the folks on *Last Stand* who might come with her for a tactical assault like this. Laney was smooth. Tessa competent. In the end, she had asked Wyatt.

If things went sideways, what Brianna really wanted was ruthless brutality. Wyatt Nakada had that in spades.

"You mind yourself out there," Tessa said to the man as the two of them stood outside the back door. "She'll give orders on this. You ask how high as you jump. Understood?"

"Got it," Wyatt said.

He glanced over at her and Brianna felt his appraisal as his eyes walked from her feet to the crown of her head. Another man might be mentally stripping her naked, but Wyatt was measuring her for lethality. That was the gleam in his eyes.

She felt herself bristle at the man and his presumptions that he was better. Her chin came up defiantly and she scowled mightily at the giant.

"Yeah," he said with a quick grin. "You'll do."

Brianna didn't know the man's backstory at all, but felt

like he had just admitted her into the sort of deadly guild he rated himself and Tessa Sladek in. One that Laney was only starting to qualify for.

Oh, buttercup, if you only knew what really *went on inside my head.*

But she grinned back instead of replying. Turned outward and nodded him into her wake.

More care was required this time, because the sun was mostly behind her, low on the horizon. Lights over there indicating that there was power, though she didn't know if they were on the ship or from the building.

She swept all the way to her left, passing around the entire town and drifting like a ghost to the edge of the landing field, where the bulk of the ship was between her and them. Stealing it still sounded like a better idea in her head, but she understood that those risks were much higher. And then they'd have to do something about the folks trapped on this planet.

She couldn't risk the authorities in this sector taking a closer look at her false credentials. Not after everything that **Constanz** had done to save her from…*those men.*

The ship was big and narrow. Still reminded her of a knife blade edge down for some reason.

They crossed beyond the tail of the ship to a small cluster of bushes growing nearby, and she settled in to listen to the music as the sun finally set behind her, turning the sky the color of blood as everything drained.

Now, the fun began. She knew how long these phonograph disks lasted, all running about the same length within a minute or so.

She turned to Wyatt.

Brianna had chosen the man because if what she had in mind failed, he might need to kill a vast number of complete strangers, in the dark, while covering her.

He called the weapon *Doomripper*. Corwin Arms G-77. 6mm select-capable assault rifle with a 24mm grenade launcher on the top, loaded with four high explosive rounds. Deadly, in the right hands.

She had watched the way he carried the weapon and understood that his were the right hands.

Brianna nodded and slipped out of her jacket, placing it just so on the ground. The white linen shirt got unbuttoned next and folded carefully to go over it. The twin chemises she had selected today went next.

Wyatt nodded when she glanced, but remained focused downrange, a soldier on watch and only occasionally enjoying the show she was putting on.

Boots and socks remained in place for now, in case she needed to run suddenly. Bad time to cut your foot on a sharp rock or step on a rusty nail. Brianna unhooked her pleated skirt and slipped it down, along with the single slip underneath, more of a loose petticoat than anything. It gave her space to move suddenly if trouble came.

Wearing only her shoes, she squatted nude next to Wyatt and listened as the symphony on the phonograph wound itself down. Roughly three minutes to conclusion.

"Are you ready?" she asked.

Wyatt grunted without looking at her nudity. She wondered if he was shy on top of everything, and the gruffness was a cover. Interesting, considering the number of women around him all the time these days.

She made a mental note to ask Constanz at some point what he might think. Or the Captain.

She'd been ogled by nearly every man she'd encountered in the last ten years, Wyatt included, but he also kept his hands and his comments to himself.

She smiled and rose, moving like a nude ghost as the darkness began to settle, turning everything gray.

This world had no moon, so darkness would be deep. That would work to her advantage.

Brianna slipped to the edge of the building. It had no windows on this side. The side with the open door had lights high up to allow indirect sun, but nothing you could see out of.

Just the inside lights spilling out from that open door.

As she reached the corner, she listened.

And smelled.

Unwashed men, playing on Fin's joke about manly men. The funk was sharper here. The sound wasn't the loud ribaldry of earlier. Perhaps folks were already settling in for the night, having drunk booze and carried on all day?

One could hope.

She peeked around the corner now.

No change from earlier, save two empty beer bottles someone had sat down next to the phonograph while changing records at some point today. Sand and dirt packed hard by traffic and not loosened up by rain. Little vegetation once you got as close as those bushes where she'd left Wyatt.

The only cover if something went wrong, which was why she'd left her boots on for this.

The symphony wound down and trailed off with a single violin note drawn slowly by an expert.

Then silence.

Brianna held herself perfectly still and watched. The sound from inside was conversations, but not boasting or roaring.

The end of a long workday, perhaps, off raiding other worlds and returning here to wait.

Something.

A shadow cast outwards at the door presaged a man emerging.

Ergrove, as before, but not the man she'd seen. Lighter

skinned than even Brianna or Wyatt. Sandy brown hair a little long and thin on top.

Rough pants the color of sand. Button-up shirt in cotton so old as to be almost formless and dingy if it had started out white. Leather vest with stains and holes.

He gave the impression of tallness, but a lanky one. Skinny. Perhaps one hundred and ninety centimeters, but hardly heavier than her.

He walked to the phonograph, nodding to himself.

Brianna slipped smoothly out from the edge of the building and stared at the man.

He looked up at motion and his jaw fell open.

Nude woman, standing all of about five meters away. That she had no hair anywhere below her neck might even make her look more spectral than normal.

Brianna held a single finger to her lips, eyes locked with the man.

He blinked. Again. Jaw fallen open wide enough to catch flies.

Brianna had no doubt that Wyatt was lined up and prepared to kill the man.

No, Wyatt probably assumed that she would handle one man, and was prepared to fire a grenade into the door as a party favor, then shoot anyone emerging afterwards.

She smiled invitingly at the stranger, still demanding silence with her eyes.

Brianna's other hand beckoned the man closer in a slow, negligent way she hoped he would remember as ghost-like later.

Something finally connected in his head. The man took a single, stumbling step towards her, then stopped.

She watched him glance back over a shoulder, as if wondering whether he should say anything.

Brianna took a half-step back, as though perhaps the thought of others seeing a ghost would cause her to vanish.

And it put her in a position to duck around the corner and run like hell if he suddenly decided to invite everyone else to see a nude woman.

The man looked back at her and Brianna smiled. Blew him a silent kiss invitingly.

He staggered like a stunned cow and took another step forward, lechery and wonder at war in his eyes.

Brianna slid backwards another half step, drawing him in her wake, finger to her lips in the universal sign of silence.

He nodded and followed.

She let the man draw close, then stopped him with a hand on his chest when she had him where she wanted him. He paused, confused. Dazed. Something.

Brianna puckered her lips and leaned forward, inviting a first kiss before any rough thoughts occurred to the man. She had a plan.

Ghosts haunting a ghost town.

The man leaned carefully forward, hands down by his sides as if she was a soap bubble that might pop if he touched her.

Rough lips. Not a good kisser. Not the point. He closed his eyes to enjoy the moment.

Brianna chopped him on both sides of the neck, right below and behind the ears.

Stranger went out like a light, collapsing forward.

She didn't catch him, but slowed his fall, dragging him out of sight around the corner.

He'd be unconscious for a time, and the last memory when he woke up was a kiss from a naked fairy.

Or a ghost.

Brianna leaned to the corner and looked. Nobody. No change in the sound, either.

She slipped around the corner, staying close to the wall.

The phonograph box was about sixty centimeters on a side, and roughly thirty tall. Wood case she could close, with a nifty space on the top where it held a dozen records in a carrier, so that the two always traveled together.

She worked quickly, pulling the record up and slipping it into its case, then into the carrier, latching it shut. The lid folded silently down and latched into place as well, on either side of a carrying handle.

Brianna lifted it. Not too heavy, but nothing she wanted to run with in one hand. Still, a ghost had come and stolen their phonograph before disappearing.

Maybe the planet was inhabited? Maybe it was just ghosts…

The man tending the phonograph would have to decide what kind of story he told his fellows when he woke up.

She circled back to the bush where Wyatt was hunched down and aiming *Doomripper*. Resting the phonograph for a moment, Brianna folded up all her clothes into a bundle in her other hand, and they moved.

Wyatt made almost no sound. Brianna huffed slightly from the weight, unaccustomed to the bulk on one hip.

Still, they got back to the others quickly.

Fin's mouth dropped open when he realized that he was looking at a nude ghost, but he shook his head once to clear it and turned to a grinning Tessa Sladek.

"You are a most evil woman," Abigail grinned as she took the weight of the phonograph from Brianna's hands.

Brianna grinned back and started to dress. It only took moments, and the others had all gathered outside the back door. Wyatt pulled it shut and they moved down the alleyway, or the back. Whatever term you used to describe the back of a building where town faded into yards and then grasslands.

The vehicle was where Fin had left it. They piled in quickly and drove off, heading upriver until Fin found bare stone, where he turned and raced madly.

Night was falling quickly, but the man seemed to see in the dark as well as the day, hardly jarring them with bumps, let alone having to drive around trees.

They made it back to the ship and boarded. Brianna mostly stood around as Fin and Tessa explained things to Auntie. Then everyone was in motion.

Brianna found herself swept along to the kitchen, where Abigail started the big pot for boiling water.

Brianna ended up seated across from Wyatt.

He had cold, appraising eyes, but a smile appeared, if only for a moment.

"At least he got a kiss for his trouble," the man said.

Then he clammed up and didn't speak again until they were in orbit.

Scene Eighteen

Tessa relaxed under an awning Fin had stretched out from the cargo bay, watching the crowd ebb and flow around them.

Parth City was in the middle of fall, and a heavy mist was drifting like fog across the small town.

Auntie was taking a turn at the stall, dickering with locals over prices and trade items to swap. They'd been here three days, and the mayor had declared today a holiday, sending riders and folks running to some of the outlying communities with news of a ship with the sorts of supplies that *Last Stand* had brought with them.

That had turned into a carnival, of sorts, in spite of the oppressive dampness that shrouded everything.

"I'm sorry about *Lacot*," Tessa said to Fin, sitting in a folding canvas chair identical to hers while people watching.

"Oh, I think it turned out pretty good," he replied, turning to grin at her. "We had an adventure. Robbed some folks. And contributed to ghost stories. How many people get to say that?"

"Should we tell Bao Li or someone about the place?"

"Not until we have a chance to go back and look around for more stuff to steal," he said mischievously. "And bring our resident ghost. Or worse, several of you might do it next time, and we can try to convince them that a coven of witches is angry at their mere presence. Think of the silly fun we could have with six of you running around wearing nothing but boots."

She grinned and shook her head.

"You're just looking for an excuse to get me naked," she observed.

"Guilty," he grinned back. "Hell, I'd drag you back inside right now and let you have your way with me, but I'm kinda enjoying the energy I'm absorbing from the crowd. Not often we get to be heroes, ya know?"

She nodded. It was a nice feeling. Abigail would get up on stage in the local auditorium later tonight and put on a one-woman show, after everyone had had a chance to buy and sell.

Wasn't even just *Last Stand,* either. Other folks had seen the makings of a party and brought goods to town to sell, so there were tables covering most of a hectare right now. Some fresh fruit, but a lot of cans. Plants and seeds. Cloth and clothing.

The knitting patterns might have been printed on iridium plates for the way folks pounced on them. Abigail had limited everyone to buying exactly one, with the understanding that those would all get traded around later, after *Last Stand* had gone home.

Or wherever they were going next. Wasn't home. Home was three meters behind her, a battered, old, Randovall Nucleonautics Light Tumbrel with a Zaddinul soul that would never surrender. Pain in the ass, some days, but full of love for the folks who cared about it.

Auntie was laughing with someone. Middle-aged

woman. They hugged and more jars and sleeves changed hands.

Parth was cash poor. Rich in people. Rich in trade, when you could swap things. And *Last Stand* had been the catalyst for something like a country fair. Even Abigail was being paid in goods tonight, instead of coin.

They might not make much money when it was all said and done, but they'd break even plus a little.

Mostly because they weren't treating these folks like a captive market they could bleed dry.

She wanted to come back here occasionally. Swing by MacGeorge's shop and clean the man out, then head here. Maybe in the spring, when seeds and rootlings would be in demand.

Not every job had to be a crime in the making. Too much of that right now, but mostly because Ergrove and Lorastir had a hard grip on the throats of society, and had expensive aristocrats to maintain.

Regular folk didn't have many options. Lots of them had turned to criminal enterprises. In that, she supposed those men on *Lacot* were just her, with a bigger ship and a different approach to surviving.

Still, one of these days, she needed to hit them with more ghosts. And maybe a coven of nude, angry witches, just to really mess with their minds.

Tessa laughed out loud and stood up. Fin looked up expectantly, then took her hand when she held it out.

She pulled him to his feet.

"What's up, beautiful?" he asked.

"You're getting me naked," she grinned down at him. "And reminding me why I put up with you."

"Work, work, work," he nodded, grinning back at her.

"Auntie," she yelled, causing Marusya to look back. "You're in charge."

Maru rolled her eyes when she realized where Tessa and Fin were headed, then nodded.

Maybe she'd find someone to spend some time with here as well. Marusya Kuznetsov had lost a husband and four children to a generation of war, with Tessa being her only blood relation left these days.

They all deserved a little happiness. She'd found herself a unicorn and was keeping him.

Days like this—planets like this—reminded her that it was good to be alive.

Read More

Be sure to read the rest of the Last Stand series!

https://www.knottedroadpress.com/product-category/last-stand

About the Author

Blaze Ward writes science fiction in the Alexandria Station universe (Jessica Keller, The Science Officer, The Story Road, etc.) as well as several other science fiction universes, such as Star Dragon, the Dominion, and more. He also writes odd bits of high fantasy with swords and orcs. In addition, he is the Editor and Publisher of *Boundary Shock Quarterly Magazine*. You can find out more at his website www.blazeward.com, as well as Facebook, Goodreads, and other places.

Blaze's works are available as ebooks, paper, and audio, and can be found at a variety of online vendors. His newsletter comes out regularly, and you can also follow his blog on his website. He really enjoys interacting with fans, and looks forward to any and all questions—even ones about his books!

Never miss a release!

If you'd like to be notified of new releases, sign up for my newsletter.

http://www.blazeward.com/newsletter/

Buy More!

Did you know that you can buy directly from the KRP website?

https://www.knottedroadpress.com/shop/

Connect with Blaze!

Web: www.blazeward.com
Boundary Shock Quarterly (BSQ):
https://www.boundaryshockquarterly.com/

About Knotted Road Press

Knotted Road Press publishes dynamic fiction set in exotic locations and unique non-fiction voices in genres such as autobiography, business, cookbooks, and how-to. Our authors cover a wide range of genres including science fiction, fantasy, mystery, literary, and poetry, appealing to all readers. We offer both DRM-free ebooks and print books for a global readership.

Knotted Road Press
www.KnottedRoadPress.com
www.KnottedRoadPress.com/Shop